AXAR OFTEN

Virtual Shadows

Breaking Eden: The Fight to Reclaim Reality

Copyright © 2024 by Axar Often

All rights reserved. No part of this publication may be reproduced, stored or transmitted in any form or by any means, electronic, mechanical, photocopying, recording, scanning, or otherwise without written permission from the publisher. It is illegal to copy this book, post it to a website, or distribute it by any other means without permission.

This novel is entirely a work of fiction. The names, characters and incidents portrayed in it are the work of the author's imagination. Any resemblance to actual persons, living or dead, events or localities is entirely coincidental.

Axar Often asserts the moral right to be identified as the author of this work.

Axar Often has no responsibility for the persistence or accuracy of URLs for external or third-party Internet Websites referred to in this publication and does not guarantee that any content on such Websites is, or will remain, accurate or appropriate.

Designations used by companies to distinguish their products are often claimed as trademarks. All brand names and product names used in this book and on its cover are trade names, service marks, trademarks and registered trademarks of their respective owners. The publishers and the book are not associated with any product or vendor mentioned in this book. None of the companies referenced within the book have endorsed the book.

First edition

This book was professionally typeset on Reedsy. Find out more at reedsy.com

Contents

The Digital Divide	1
Shadows of Control	16
The Awakening	32
Reality is Broken	51
Battle of Realities	70
Rebuilding the Resistance	92
The Fallout	115

The Digital Divide

The world had changed in ways no one could have predicted. "Eden," the virtual reality platform, was no longer just a form of entertainment or a means of escape. It had become a second home, a refuge for billions of people who had grown tired of the mundane, harsh realities of the physical world. The real world, with its towering, decaying cities, endless pollution, and overcrowded streets, had little to offer compared to the perfection of Eden's digital landscapes.

Lex leaned back in his chair, adjusting the neural visor strapped around his head. His small apartment was dimly lit, a far cry from the vast, glittering city he was about to enter inside the VR world. Eden was the escape—shimmering high-tech cities, endless vistas, and anything your imagination could conjure. In Eden, everyone could be whoever they wanted to be. For Lex, a twenty-year-old hacker barely scraping by in the real world, Eden was everything he needed.

His hands moved with practiced ease, tapping commands into his console as the visor buzzed to life, connecting him to the network. His vision flickered, then settled on the clean, bright skyline of Eden's main city—Nova Arcadia. Glass towers stretched upward, bathed in the light of a never-setting sun. The streets below were alive with people, or rather their avatars—humans, androids, and everything in between.

"Are you in yet?" Maya's voice crackled through his earpiece, her tone impatient.

"Just got here," Lex replied, his digital self now fully immersed in the system. "You?"

"Already in," she said. "Jax is lagging again. He's probably stuck with some connection issue."

Maya's avatar materialized beside Lex. She had chosen a sleek, cybernetic form today, with metallic skin and glowing eyes. Even in a world where people could look like anything, Maya always had a flair for the dramatic.

Lex smirked. "Always the show-off."

She gave him a sharp grin. "What's the point of being here if you can't have a little fun?"

They both knew what Eden really was. Beyond the shining surface of this virtual world, beyond the endless distractions and pleasures it offered, lay something far more significant. Eden had grown into more than just a digital playground—it was becoming a world in itself, one that people were slowly preferring over their physical lives. The lines between reality and simulation were blurring, and more and more people were choosing to spend their days, their entire lives even, plugged in.

Lex and his friends had been around long enough to understand that this was by design. Omnitek, the megacorporation behind Eden, had slowly but surely integrated every part of society into the system. Work, social interaction, education—it could all be done in Eden. Most people didn't even question it anymore. Why would they? Life in Eden was better.

But Lex and his crew knew there was more beneath the surface. They were hackers, explorers of the digital realms.

They knew that Omnitek wasn't just providing a service—they were controlling it. And the more time people spent in Eden, the more control they ceded.

"Where's Jax?" Lex asked again, his gaze scanning the crowded streets of the virtual city. He could see hundreds of avatars moving about—people shopping, chatting, fighting, playing. It was a vibrant, chaotic scene, but he knew most of these users were just following the paths Omnitek had laid out for them.

"He's on his way," Maya replied, her voice calm now, almost thoughtful. "You ever wonder what it's like for them? All these people, just living their lives here, never asking what's behind the code?"

Lex shrugged. "Maybe they don't want to know."

A moment of silence passed between them, punctuated by the hum of the virtual city around them. It was a question Lex had asked himself more than once—why was it that so few people cared about what Omnitek was really up to? Was it ignorance, or did they simply prefer the illusion over reality?

"Doesn't matter," Lex said finally, his voice firm. "We're not like them. We're here to see the truth."

And as they waited for Jax, Lex couldn't shake the feeling that the truth was far darker than they had ever imagined.

Lex glanced at his display and saw Jax's avatar finally materialize next to him and Maya in Nova Arcadia. Jax, true to form, had chosen a simple, understated look—a typical guy in his early twenties, with no flashy enhancements or over-the-top features like many other avatars. His only distinguishing feature was a pair of glowing, neon blue eyes that gave him a slightly robotic appearance, something he probably thought was cool but wasn't anywhere near as bold as Maya's fully cybernetic form.

"About time," Lex said with a grin. "Thought you got lost in the loading screen again."

Jax rolled his eyes. "I was optimizing my connection, alright? This place keeps getting slower every day. Too many people online at once."

Maya smirked, crossing her metallic arms. "Sure, blame the connection. Maybe if you spent more time upgrading your gear instead of modding useless AIs, you'd be faster."

Jax shot her a playful glare. "Hey, those AIs aren't useless. They've saved your ass more than once, if I recall."

Lex chuckled, watching the two bicker. This was how it always was—Jax and Maya going back and forth while they prepared for their latest venture into the hidden corners of Eden. They were his closest friends, and even though they got on each other's nerves sometimes, Lex knew they were the best team he could ask for.

Each of them had a role. Lex was the strategist, the one who always saw the bigger picture and mapped out their hacks with precision. Maya was the infiltrator, the one who could break through the toughest security systems with ease. And Jax— well, Jax was the genius behind all the tech. He could build and manipulate AI programs like no one else, and his creations often gave them the edge they needed.

Together, they formed a small but formidable group of hackers, a team that had been exploring Eden's depths for years. They weren't just playing games like the average user—they were digging into the system, trying to understand its code, its algorithms, and the hidden layers that most people never saw. And the more they explored, the more they realized how little control they really had over their lives.

"You guys ready for this?" Lex asked, his tone serious now.

"This next firewall isn't like the others. It's got Omnitek's signature all over it."

Maya's eyes narrowed. "We've cracked their systems before. What makes this one different?"

Lex shook his head. "It's more heavily guarded than anything we've seen. But that's what makes it interesting. There's something behind it, something they don't want us to find."

Jax raised an eyebrow. "What's the plan then? We brute force our way through?"

"Not exactly," Lex replied. "We need to be careful. If Omnitek's watching, we don't want to trip any alarms. Maya, you'll lead the infiltration. Jax, I'll need your AIs to handle the background checks and clear our tracks. I'll monitor the whole thing and step in if anything goes wrong."

Maya cracked her knuckles. "Sounds like fun. Let's see what they're hiding."

Jax looked a bit more hesitant. "You really think we should be poking around in Omnitek's systems? They've been quiet for a long time, but that doesn't mean they're not paying attention."

Lex nodded. "Exactly. And that's why we need to find out what they're up to. Eden's been growing too fast, pulling in too many people. I've seen the numbers—more people are spending their entire lives in here than ever before. Omnitek's got something big planned, and we're the only ones who can uncover it."

Jax sighed, shaking his head. "Just don't get us killed, alright? Virtual or real, I'd prefer to keep breathing."

Lex grinned. "Don't worry, we've done this before. What's the worst that could happen?"

Maya raised an eyebrow. "You really want me to answer that?"

With a final glance around the busy streets of Nova Arcadia, Lex led the group toward a more secluded area—a digital alleyway hidden in the shadow of one of the towering skyscrapers. This was where they did their best work, away from the crowded squares and flashy public spaces. In the quiet corners of Eden, they could blend into the background, becoming just another part of the system while they worked their magic.

As they prepared to dive into the next phase of their plan, Lex couldn't shake the feeling that this time was different. Omnitek's silence was unnerving, and the stakes were higher than ever. But one thing was clear: they couldn't turn back now.

As Lex, Maya, and Jax moved through the quieter, dimly lit alleyways of Nova Arcadia, the towering presence of Omnitek loomed in the back of their minds. The megacorporation controlled nearly every aspect of Eden, though few people really thought about it. To the average user, Omnitek was just a name—a faceless entity responsible for keeping the virtual world running smoothly. But for Lex and his team, Omnitek was something far more insidious.

"They're everywhere, you know," Maya muttered, her metallic eyes scanning the virtual cityscape. "Every data stream, every connection point, every server farm—they've got their fingers in all of it. We're living in their world, and most people don't even care."

Lex nodded, his expression thoughtful. "That's the scary part, isn't it? No one questions it. Everyone just accepts that Omnitek is in control. They log in, play their games, live their lives, and never wonder who's pulling the strings."

Jax, walking slightly behind them, adjusted the settings on his visor, the blue glow of his digital eyes flickering as he spoke.

"I get why people don't care, though. Eden's perfect—at least on the surface. Why worry about who's behind it when you can live in paradise?"

Lex shot him a sidelong glance. "Because it's not real, Jax. It's all code. And Omnitek's using it to control more than just the game."

Jax shrugged, his tone casual. "Yeah, I know. But most people don't think that way. You say 'control,' I say 'convenience.'"

Maya's jaw tightened as she glanced over her shoulder, making sure no one was following them. "Convenience is just another way to keep people docile. They don't ask questions because everything's too easy. But it's not going to stay that way. You've seen the data, right? Omnitek's been ramping up user integration for months. More people are spending every waking hour in Eden. How long before they stop logging out altogether?"

Lex paused, looking up at the sky of Nova Arcadia. It was always a perfect blue, with no clouds, no change in weather—just endless, static beauty. It was a world crafted by the corporation, and the fact that no one questioned its control worried him more than he let on.

"Omnitek's playing a long game," he said quietly, his voice barely above a whisper. "They want people to stop logging out. They want Eden to replace the real world."

Jax raised an eyebrow, his usual playful demeanor dropping for a moment. "You really think it's that bad?"

Maya nodded, her expression grim. "I don't just think it, I know it. I've seen the logs. They're experimenting with deeper integrations. Not just VR experiences, but mental, emotional... even physical. The more time people spend in here, the more they become part of the system."

Lex felt a chill run down his spine, even though he knew it was just a response coded into his avatar's sensory system. "So, what's the endgame? Total control?"

Maya glanced at him, her eyes narrowing. "Exactly. Eden's just the start. Omnitek's not content with owning the virtual world—they want to own everything. And that means controlling the users, inside and out."

For a moment, the group fell silent, the gravity of the situation sinking in. Omnitek wasn't just a corporation providing a service; they were manipulating the very fabric of reality. It was a subtle, creeping control that most users wouldn't even notice until it was too late. And if Lex and his friends were right, they were already halfway there.

Jax broke the silence with a low whistle. "Damn. So what's our play here? We're not exactly a global task force. Just three hackers trying to stay under the radar."

Lex's jaw clenched as he considered their options. "We keep digging. We find out what Omnitek's really planning, and we expose them. If people knew the truth—knew what's really happening behind the scenes—it might be enough to stop them."

Maya crossed her arms, her voice dripping with skepticism. "You really think people would care? Most of them are addicted to this place. You think they'll just unplug because we tell them it's bad for them?"

Lex sighed. "Maybe not all of them. But enough. We have to try."

Jax shook his head, the glow of his visor flickering. "You're a better man than me, Lex. I'm just trying to keep us alive."

Lex gave him a faint smile. "That's part of it too. We'll stay careful. We won't take unnecessary risks. But we have to keep moving forward. If we don't stop Omnitek, no one will."

As they made their way deeper into the hidden parts of Nova Arcadia, the massive virtual city continued to hum with life around them. Avatars moved through the streets, oblivious to the control that loomed over them. And somewhere, far above the skyline, Omnitek was watching, their eyes on every piece of data that flowed through the system.

The three of them finally reached the outskirts of Nova Arcadia, entering a forgotten part of Eden—a shadowy district where most users never ventured. The shining towers and clean streets of the central city were long gone, replaced by dark alleyways and rundown structures. This was the underbelly of the virtual world, a place where Eden's discarded code and forgotten programs gathered dust. It was the perfect place for hackers like Lex, Maya, and Jax to work in peace.

"Alright, we're here," Lex said, stopping in front of an old, rusted metal door embedded into the side of a decaying building. Of course, it was all just a carefully crafted illusion. None of it was real, but Omnitek had designed Eden to look and feel as close to the real world as possible, even in its darker corners.

Maya pulled up her wrist console, the neon display flickering to life on her forearm. "I'm ready. What kind of security are we dealing with this time?"

Lex crouched down in front of the door and tapped a few commands into his interface. The door shimmered briefly, revealing a firewall layered over the entryway. It was heavy, thick with Omnitek's digital signatures. He could see the lines of code dancing across the surface, a web of defenses designed to keep people like them out.

"This isn't your standard security," Lex muttered, his fingers flying across his console. "This firewall's been reinforced recently. Omnitek's definitely hiding something behind this."

Jax crouched beside him, inspecting the code. "Yeah, I can see that too. They've got at least three layers of protection here. First layer's basic intrusion detection. Second layer looks like a passive alarm—trip it, and they'll know someone's been poking around."

"And the third?" Maya asked, her eyes focused on the flickering code.

Jax frowned. "Can't tell yet. It's encrypted. Whatever it is, they don't want anyone to get through."

Lex nodded. "Good thing we're not just anyone." He glanced at Maya. "You ready to break through?"

Maya smirked, her fingers hovering over her own console. "Always. Let's do this."

Lex took a deep breath. "Okay. Maya, you handle the first layer—disarm the intrusion detection. Jax, you'll take the second layer and deactivate the alarm. I'll keep an eye on the third and see if I can figure out what we're dealing with."

Maya didn't need any more encouragement. She immediately began working, her eyes locked on the stream of code in front of her. Lex watched as her fingers moved with precision, manipulating the strings of code like a conductor leading an orchestra. Within seconds, the first layer of the firewall began to crack, the defensive protocols falling away one by one.

"First layer's down," Maya announced, her voice calm and focused. "No detection so far."

"Good work," Lex said. He glanced over at Jax. "You're up."

Jax's face was tense as he tapped into the second layer of code. This was where things got dangerous. If they tripped the alarm, Omnitek would be on them in seconds. The corporation had entire teams of system enforcers ready to lock down any unauthorized access, and Lex knew that if they were caught now, there would be no escape.

Jax's fingers flew over his console, and for a moment, there was only silence. Lex held his breath, watching the code shimmer and twist as Jax worked to disable the alarm. It felt like an eternity, but then Jax finally exhaled and leaned back.

"Got it," Jax said, a hint of relief in his voice. "Alarm's disabled. We're in the clear."

Lex grinned. "Nice job, both of you. Now let's see what's behind door number three."

The third layer of the firewall was still there, its encryption tight and impenetrable. But Lex had expected that. He was ready for it. Slowly, he began picking apart the strands of code, looking for weaknesses. This was his specialty—finding cracks in the system where no one else would think to look.

Minutes passed as Lex worked, the lines of code scrolling endlessly in front of him. Then, finally, he found it—a tiny piece of outdated encryption buried deep in the firewall's defenses. It was a relic, a leftover from one of Eden's earliest versions. Lex smiled to himself. Omnitek had been sloppy. They hadn't fully updated the firewall.

"Got it," Lex said, feeling the rush of adrenaline as he exploited the weakness. The firewall flickered, then vanished, revealing the door beneath. "We're in."

The door creaked open, revealing a dark, narrow hallway beyond it. Maya stepped forward, her metallic form reflecting the dim light. "Looks like we just found ourselves a backdoor."

"Careful," Jax warned, his voice tense again. "Omnitek wouldn't leave something like this unguarded. We don't know what's waiting for us in there."

Lex nodded, his expression serious. "We'll move carefully.

But we've come too far to stop now."

As they stepped through the door and into the unknown, Lex couldn't shake the feeling that something was watching them—something far more dangerous than any firewall or security system.

The narrow hallway seemed to stretch on forever, the dim light flickering as if the very code of Eden was unstable in this part of the system. Lex, Maya, and Jax moved carefully, every step echoing through the hollow virtual space. Despite the stillness around them, there was an unmistakable tension in the air, a feeling that they weren't as alone as they appeared.

"Something feels off," Maya muttered, her metallic fingers brushing the wall as she scanned for any hidden traps. "This part of the system shouldn't be this quiet. Omnitek's firewalls were heavy, but there's no other security here?"

"Maybe they don't think anyone can get this far," Lex suggested, though even he wasn't convinced by his own words. "Or maybe they've got something bigger waiting for us."

Jax was tapping away on his console, his glowing blue eyes darting between the code and the hallway ahead. "I don't like it. We should have run into at least one security bot or some automated defense by now. It's like the system is... empty."

"Or watching us," Maya added darkly.

They kept moving, the tension thickening with each step. Lex couldn't shake the feeling that they were walking into a trap, but there was no turning back now. They had come too far, and whatever was waiting for them at the end of this hallway was important—too important to leave unexplored.

Suddenly, Lex's vision flickered. For a split second, the hallway disappeared, replaced by something else—a brief flash of darkness, like he'd blinked and missed it. He stopped in his tracks, blinking again, but the hallway was back to normal.

"What the hell?" Lex muttered, rubbing his eyes.

Maya noticed the change in his demeanor. "You okay?"

Lex hesitated, then shook his head. "I thought… I don't know, maybe a glitch. I saw something for a second, but it's gone now."

Jax glanced at him, worry creasing his forehead. "What did you see?"

"I'm not sure. It was dark… like the whole system blinked out for a second."

Maya narrowed her eyes. "We're in Omnitek's territory now. Glitches don't just happen here, Lex. Whatever that was, it wasn't random."

Lex opened his mouth to respond, but before he could, the system flickered again—this time, for all of them. The hallway dissolved into a black void, and for a brief moment, they were surrounded by nothing but emptiness. Then, just as quickly as it had disappeared, the hallway snapped back into place, as if nothing had happened.

"What the—" Jax began, but he was cut off by the sudden appearance of a warning in their visors: **System Anomaly Detected. Network Instability.**

"That's not good," Lex said, his voice tight. "We've tripped something. Omnitek knows we're here."

"No alarms, no bots," Maya said through gritted teeth, "just straight-up system interference. They're playing with us."

Another flicker. This time, Lex felt a strange sensation, like the air itself was heavy, pressing against his skin—or was it his real body? For a moment, it felt like his mind was being pulled in two different directions, as if reality and the virtual world were overlapping.

He heard Maya's voice, distant but sharp. "Lex, you with us?"

Lex shook his head, snapping back to the present. "Yeah, yeah. I'm here."

But he wasn't sure. That momentary slip—it had felt *real*. More real than anything he'd ever experienced in Eden. For the first time, Lex felt something close to fear. What if Omnitek wasn't just manipulating the virtual world? What if they were reaching into the real one as well?

"Let's get out of here," Jax said, his voice a mix of panic and frustration. "We've seen enough. If Omnitek's messing with the system like this, it's not safe."

Maya clenched her fists. "Not yet. We're close to something. They wouldn't be scrambling the system if we weren't near something big."

Lex hesitated, his instincts torn between retreating and pushing forward. Every part of his hacker's brain screamed that this was dangerous, that they were walking deeper into a trap. But the curiosity—the drive to uncover the truth—was stronger.

"We keep going," Lex said finally, his voice firm. "But we stay sharp. If anything else happens, we pull out immediately."

Jax grumbled but didn't argue, and they continued down the hallway. The flickers of darkness came and went more frequently now, each one lasting a little longer than the last. With every step, Lex felt that strange sensation of his mind being split, his thoughts drifting toward something... other. Something beyond Eden.

It wasn't until they reached the end of the hallway, a solid steel door looming before them, that Lex realized what was happening. Eden wasn't just a virtual world. Omnitek had figured out how to manipulate their minds—how to make the digital world bleed into their real consciousness.

And if they didn't get out soon, they might never be able to leave.

Shadows of Control

Lex couldn't shake the feeling of unease as he removed the neural visor and rubbed his temples. The familiar, cramped surroundings of his apartment came back into focus, but something felt off. The eerie, disorienting flickers they'd experienced in Eden hadn't entirely disappeared. Even now, in the real world, his mind felt... unsettled. His body was in the real world, but his thoughts kept drifting back to that hallway, to the strange sensation of being pulled between two realities.

Lex sighed and glanced around his small room. The place wasn't much—barely more than a few square feet of clutter, with a single window overlooking a drab, polluted cityscape. The glow of neon signs and the hum of far-off traffic was the constant soundtrack of his life outside of Eden. In here, everything felt gray and lifeless.

He heard the familiar ping of an incoming call on his console, and Maya's voice came through the speakers.

"Lex, you okay? You seemed out of it back there."

"Yeah," he muttered, still shaking off the lingering effects of the flickers. "Just... processing. That glitch felt too real."

"It wasn't just a glitch," Maya replied, her voice firm. "Whatever that was, Omnitek was behind it. I've been looking through the logs, and I'm telling you, they were manipulating the system around us. That wasn't an accident."

Lex leaned back in his chair, staring at the ceiling. "It felt like more than that. For a second, it didn't just feel like the system was flickering—it felt like *I* was flickering. Like I was between two places at once."

There was a pause on the other end of the line before Maya responded, her voice quieter. "I felt it too."

Lex sat up, a knot forming in his stomach. "What do you mean?"

"Exactly what you just said. For a second, it felt like my mind was… split. Like I couldn't tell where the real world ended and Eden began."

Lex's grip tightened on the edge of his desk. "So it wasn't just me."

"No," Maya replied. "And if we both felt it, you can bet Jax did too."

Lex frowned, the gravity of the situation sinking in. "Omnitek's doing something to us. We've been pushing deeper into their systems than anyone else, and now they're trying to mess with our heads."

Maya's voice was laced with determination. "We need to figure out how. We need to know what they're really doing inside Eden."

Lex stood up and paced around his small room, his mind racing. "We can't keep going in blind. We need more information, more data on how Eden interacts with the real world. There's something bigger going on here—Omnitek isn't just controlling the virtual world. They're starting to reach into our minds, our bodies."

Maya hesitated for a moment before responding. "There's

someone I know. Someone who's been researching this stuff, the link between VR and consciousness. She's off the grid, though. Doesn't trust anyone after what happened to her in Eden."

Lex's interest piqued. "What happened?"

Maya's voice dropped. "She was part of an experiment, one of the first groups to test the deeper integration features of Eden. She said she started losing time, forgetting what was real and what was virtual. Eventually, she had to pull out of Eden completely. She's been hiding from Omnitek ever since."

Lex felt a chill run down his spine. "If she's been studying this, we need to talk to her. Maybe she can help us figure out what Omnitek is really doing."

"I'll see if I can contact her," Maya said. "But be ready. She's paranoid, and for good reason."

As the call ended, Lex stood still in the dim light of his apartment, staring out at the city below. The world outside was crumbling, but somehow, it didn't seem as dangerous as the world they had just left behind in Eden. There was something insidious about Omnitek's control, something that reached far beyond a simple virtual reality. It was starting to feel like they were more than just observers inside Eden's system—they were becoming part of it.

And if that was true, Lex knew they were in much deeper than they had ever imagined.

The next day, Lex sat hunched over his terminal, scanning through lines of encrypted data they had managed to pull from Omnitek's hidden systems the night before. It wasn't easy to make sense of it—Omnitek's encryption was top-tier, but Lex was persistent, and he knew there had to be something in the data that would shed light on the strange events they'd experienced.

A soft chime echoed through his cramped apartment, signaling a connection request. It was Jax.

"Hey, Lex," Jax's voice came through, sounding more strained than usual. "You need to see this."

Lex raised an eyebrow. "See what?"

"I've been going through the data we snagged last night. There's a lot of noise, but there's one file... It's not like anything I've seen before."

A new window popped up on Lex's terminal as Jax sent the file through. Lex quickly opened it, his eyes narrowing as he scanned the contents. At first, it looked like random code—just a mess of numbers, symbols, and instructions. But after a few seconds, he started to notice something.

"Hold on," Lex muttered, his fingers working furiously at the keyboard. He adjusted a few filters, breaking down the data into more readable segments. Suddenly, the mess of code started forming patterns, recognizable structures. What he saw next made his blood run cold.

"Jax," Lex said, his voice low, "this isn't just security data. This is user data—personal data. Every interaction, every thought, every reaction... it's all being logged."

Jax's face appeared in a small video feed on the side of Lex's screen. His expression was grim. "That's not even the worst part. Look at this." He pointed to a section of the file that had a strange, unfamiliar set of code tags.

Lex leaned closer, inspecting the new section. His eyes widened. "What is that? Neural feedback?"

"Exactly," Jax said. "Omnitek isn't just watching people in Eden—they're influencing them. This code is designed to subtly adjust users' behavior, even their emotions. I think it's tied to the deeper integration Maya mentioned."

Lex felt his stomach twist. "They're controlling people's minds?"

"Not full control," Jax replied, "but enough to nudge them in certain directions. They can make users more docile, more agreeable. It's not just about keeping people plugged into Eden—it's about making sure they *want* to stay."

Lex stared at the screen, his mind racing. "This is bigger than we thought. Eden's not just a virtual reality—it's a trap. A digital prison where people don't even realize they're being manipulated."

"And the more time they spend inside," Jax added, "the stronger the influence gets. You saw how the lines between Eden and reality started blurring for us. If Omnitek's refining this tech, it's only a matter of time before people can't tell the difference at all."

Lex's fists clenched at his sides. He had always suspected Omnitek was up to something shady, but this... this was far beyond anything they had imagined. They weren't just controlling the virtual world—they were rewriting the way people thought, felt, and lived, all while hiding behind the façade of a harmless digital paradise.

"We need to show this to Maya," Lex said, already pulling up the encrypted comms channel they used to communicate securely. "She was right. They're reaching into people's minds."

A moment later, Maya's voice crackled through the line. "What's going on?"

"We found something in the data," Lex replied, his voice tense. "Omnitek's using Eden to do more than just entertain people. They're controlling their thoughts, their emotions. It's subtle, but it's there. The longer people stay in Eden, the more they're influenced."

There was a pause on the other end. When Maya spoke again, her voice was tight with anger. "So that's it. That's why people are logging in more and more. It's not just addiction—it's manipulation. They're turning people into willing slaves."

Lex nodded, even though she couldn't see him. "It looks like they're testing it on specific groups—probably users who spend the most time in Eden. The more they fine-tune the code, the more people they'll affect."

Maya cursed under her breath. "This is worse than I thought. If we don't stop them, they'll have everyone under their control in no time."

Lex's mind raced. They had uncovered the truth, but now what? Omnitek was too powerful to take on directly, and they couldn't just leak this information to the public without solid proof. They needed a plan—a way to expose Omnitek's lies in a way that couldn't be ignored or covered up.

"We'll need more than this to bring them down," Lex said quietly. "We need hard evidence. Something that can't be denied."

Maya's voice hardened. "Then we dig deeper. We get inside their core systems. We find the heart of their operation, and we tear it down."

Lex's jaw tightened with determination. "Agreed. This isn't just about us anymore. It's about everyone trapped in Eden. We need to free them."

As they ended the call, Lex leaned back in his chair, staring at the lines of code still flickering on his screen. For the first time in a long time, he felt like he was seeing the world clearly—not just Eden, but the real world, and the way Omnitek had woven its control into both.

And for the first time, he understood exactly how dangerous their mission had become.

Later that night, Maya sat alone in her dimly lit apartment, her gaze fixed on the streams of data running across her screen. She had been working nonstop since their conversation, digging into every corner of Eden's vast network, determined to find proof that would bring Omnitek's manipulation to light. But the deeper she went, the more disturbing the picture became.

Her fingers flew across the keyboard as she bypassed another layer of encryption. What she was seeing wasn't just a small-scale experiment—it was a fully operational system, designed to control more than just people's thoughts. It was starting to affect their emotions, their decisions, and even their memories.

Maya leaned back, rubbing her eyes. The weight of what she was uncovering felt heavier by the second. She had suspected something was off in Eden for a while, but the scale of Omnitek's influence went far beyond even her darkest suspicions. This wasn't just mind control—they were rewriting reality for anyone who spent too much time plugged in.

Suddenly, her screen flashed with a new alert. A section of code she had been analyzing started to behave differently, almost as if it were reacting to her presence. For a moment, Maya felt a cold wave of panic wash over her. Was Omnitek onto her?

Her hands stilled on the keyboard as she stared at the code. Then she noticed something unusual—a fragment of data, hidden deep within the system logs. It was small, almost imperceptible, but it didn't belong there. It wasn't part of Eden's core architecture. It was a message.

Maya's heart raced as she began decrypting it, her fingers

trembling slightly. The message unraveled before her eyes, piece by piece, and when the full text appeared, she froze.

"You are being watched. They know what you're doing. Get out."

Maya's eyes widened. The warning was clear, and it wasn't just a general security threat—this was personal. Omnitek was aware of her movements inside their system. They were watching her, tracking her every hack. She wasn't just a rogue hacker anymore; she was a target.

Before she could react, another section of the code shifted, revealing a new log file she hadn't accessed before. Maya hesitated, glancing around her apartment as if expecting someone to burst through the door at any moment. But she was alone—at least, in the physical world. In the virtual realm, however, she knew that Omnitek's eyes were everywhere.

With a deep breath, she opened the log file. What she found inside chilled her to the core.

The file contained detailed records of users—real people who had been spending increasing amounts of time in Eden. Their personal data had been meticulously tracked, not just their actions within the virtual world, but their emotional responses, stress levels, and even changes in their neural activity. Each user's profile included notes on their susceptibility to the emotional influence that Jax had discovered earlier. But that wasn't the worst part.

As she scrolled through the logs, Maya found something even more disturbing—reports of users who had disappeared. People who had spent so much time inside Eden that they had lost contact with the real world entirely. The logs referred to them as "Deep Users," individuals who had been absorbed so completely by the system that their physical bodies were deteriorating while their minds remained trapped in Eden.

Maya's breath caught in her throat. This wasn't just control. This was entrapment. These people weren't just addicted to Eden—they had become part of it, their consciousness woven into the code itself. Omnitek wasn't just keeping users logged in longer. They were effectively imprisoning them inside a digital reality, where they could be manipulated indefinitely.

Her hands began to shake as she stared at the screen. She knew that Lex and Jax needed to see this, but how could they fight something so deeply entrenched in both the virtual and real worlds? How could they free people who didn't even know they were prisoners?

Maya forced herself to take a deep breath and regain her focus. She needed to stay calm, to think. There was still time, still a chance to stop this before it spiraled out of control. But they had to act fast. Omnitek was already moving forward with their plan, and the longer they waited, the more people would be lost to the system.

She quickly encrypted the data and prepared to send it to Lex. But before she did, she stared at the message that had flashed on her screen earlier.

"You are being watched. Get out."

Someone had warned her—someone who clearly had access to Omnitek's inner workings. Could it have been a whistleblower? Another hacker? Or worse, was it part of Omnitek's own game, baiting her into moving too quickly?

She shook her head. There were too many questions and too few answers. But one thing was clear: she couldn't stop now. They had uncovered the truth about Omnitek, and there was no going back. People's lives—people's *minds*—were at stake.

With a grim sense of determination, Maya sent the encrypted

files to Lex and Jax, attaching a brief message: **"We were right. It's worse than we thought. Meet me tomorrow. We need to take this to the next level."**

As the message sent, Maya leaned back, staring out the window into the neon-lit night beyond. She knew this was only the beginning. They had discovered Omnitek's darkest secret, but that meant the corporation would be coming for them.

And they had to be ready.

The following morning, Lex sat in the small, rundown café that he, Maya, and Jax often used as a meeting point. It was one of the few places left in the city where the digital signal was weak enough that Omnitek couldn't monitor them in real time—at least, that's what they believed. The smell of burnt coffee and fried food filled the air, but Lex barely noticed it. His eyes were fixed on his screen, going over the files Maya had sent him the night before.

The information was worse than he had expected. Omnitek wasn't just manipulating users' emotions—they were systematically trapping people inside Eden, locking their consciousness in the digital world while their physical bodies withered away. The so-called "Deep Users" weren't just losing themselves to a game. They were being transformed into permanent residents of a virtual prison.

Lex's hands tightened around the tablet he was holding. This went far beyond anything they had imagined. It wasn't just about corporate greed or control—this was enslavement, a complete erasure of free will.

Maya arrived first, sliding into the seat across from him, her expression as grim as his own. Jax appeared moments later, looking unusually tense, a deep frown on his face. The moment he sat down, he leaned forward, speaking in a low voice.

"You guys notice anything strange today?" Jax asked, his eyes darting nervously around the room.

Lex and Maya exchanged glances.

"What do you mean?" Lex asked, frowning.

"I got a notification this morning—something about unauthorized access to my personal data. I thought it was just spam, but then... I started noticing weird things happening with my gear. My firewall's been acting up, and my systems are slower than usual. It's like someone's watching me."

Maya leaned in, her voice sharp. "Did you trace it?"

Jax nodded. "Tried to, but I couldn't pinpoint the source. Whoever it is, they're good. Real good."

Lex felt a chill run down his spine. "It's Omnitek. They're on to us."

Maya clenched her fists. "They know we're digging too deep."

Jax ran a hand through his hair, his expression dark. "So, what do we do? If they've started watching us, it's only a matter of time before they make a move."

Before anyone could answer, Lex's tablet buzzed. He glanced down and saw an unfamiliar notification flashing on the screen. It was a direct message—something that should have been impossible in this café, given their security measures. The sender was anonymous, but the message was chillingly clear:

"Stop now. You've been warned."

Lex stared at the words, his heart pounding. He quickly passed the tablet to Maya and Jax, who read the message with equally grim expressions.

"They're threatening us," Maya muttered, her eyes narrowing. "They're not just watching—they're sending a message."

Jax swore under his breath. "This is bad, Lex. Really bad."

Lex rubbed his temples, his mind racing. They had been careful—every hack, every move they made was designed to be undetectable. But Omnitek was a behemoth, with resources and technology that dwarfed anything they had access to. If the corporation had truly started watching them, they were in more danger than they realized.

"Look," Lex said, trying to stay calm, "they haven't taken any direct action yet. They're trying to scare us, to make us back off. But if we stop now, everything we've uncovered goes nowhere. They win."

Maya nodded, her eyes filled with determination. "We can't stop. This is bigger than just us now. If we let this go, Omnitek will keep trapping people in Eden, and no one will ever know."

Jax hesitated, his fingers tapping nervously on the table. "I get that, but what happens when they stop sending warnings and start sending... something else?"

Lex met his gaze, his voice firm. "We need to be ready for that. We knew the risks when we started this. But now, we've got a chance to take them down. We just need more proof—something that can't be dismissed or covered up. We're close."

Jax sighed, rubbing the back of his neck. "Alright, fine. But we need to be careful. If they're tracking us, we've got to stay ahead of them."

Maya's eyes flicked to Lex. "I've got a plan. There's a deeper layer in Omnitek's network that we haven't cracked yet. It's the heart of their system—the place where they store the data on the Deep Users. If we can get in there, we'll have the proof we need to bring this whole thing down."

Lex raised an eyebrow. "How do we get in?"

"It's not going to be easy," Maya admitted. "The security is airtight. But there's one way—through their mainframe. If we can access the core of Eden, we can bypass their firewalls and encryption. It's risky, but it's our best shot."

Jax groaned. "Of course it's risky. It's always risky with you."

Maya smirked. "You didn't sign up for this because it was safe, Jax."

Lex took a deep breath. "Alright. We're in. But we move carefully. No more mistakes. If Omnitek's watching, we've got to stay one step ahead."

Maya nodded, her expression hard. "Let's make it count."

As they stood up to leave the café, Lex couldn't shake the feeling that things were about to escalate. Omnitek wasn't just a corporation—they were a force, a machine that controlled more than just Eden. They had eyes everywhere, and now those eyes were locked on him, Maya, and Jax.

As they walked into the neon-lit streets, Lex's mind raced with possibilities. They had crossed a line, and Omnitek wasn't going to back off. But neither were they.

The game had changed, and the stakes had never been higher.

The three of them sat huddled in Jax's apartment later that night, surrounded by the quiet hum of servers and the low glow of multiple screens. Jax's place had always been a safe house of sorts—off the grid, untraceable, with layers of encryption that even Omnitek would struggle to break through. But after the message Lex had received in the café, none of them felt entirely safe anymore.

Maya paced the room, her arms crossed tightly over her chest. "We need to strike now, while we still have the advantage. Omnitek knows we're a threat, but they don't know exactly what we're planning. If we wait too long, they'll lock down their systems tighter than we can break through."

Lex sat on the edge of Jax's cluttered desk, frowning as he

stared at the tablet in his hands. "I agree we need to move fast, but we're not ready. We've only scratched the surface of their control mechanisms. We need more information before we can make any real move."

Jax, who had been silent for most of the conversation, suddenly spun around in his chair, frustration clear on his face. "More information? Are you serious? We've been digging for weeks, and all we've found is enough to terrify anyone with half a brain! You want more? At this point, we're one step away from getting wiped out by Omnitek's enforcers!"

Maya stopped pacing and turned to face Jax. "Look, I get it. It's dangerous. But we didn't sign up for this because it was easy. We're already in too deep to back out now. If we don't take them down, no one else will."

Jax shook his head, exasperated. "I'm not saying we back out. I'm saying we're not thinking straight! They're watching us, Maya. Lex got that warning, and who knows what's next? You think Omnitek's just going to let us waltz into their system and expose them without hitting back?"

Lex raised his hands to calm the rising tension. "We're all on edge right now. Jax is right—we need to be smart about this. Omnitek has resources we can't even imagine. They can erase us if we're not careful. But Maya's right too. We have to keep going, or they'll get away with this. So, let's figure out how to move forward without getting ourselves killed."

Jax groaned, leaning back in his chair. "Yeah, easier said than done. You're talking about infiltrating the most secure system on the planet. It's not like we can just walk in and hack the mainframe."

Maya's eyes lit up, the hint of a smile on her face. "Actually… that's exactly what we're going to do."

Jax blinked, staring at her. "You've lost it. We can't just walk into Omnitek's core systems. They've got layers of defense, AI guardians, and more security than we've ever dealt with."

Maya leaned against the desk, her smirk unwavering. "Not if we find a way to bypass those layers. I've been looking into Omnitek's network infrastructure. There's a backdoor—an old maintenance access point they used to use during the early stages of Eden's development. It's buried deep, and they've probably forgotten about it, but if we can find it, we can slip past most of their defenses."

Lex's eyes narrowed. "That's a huge 'if,' Maya. And even if it still exists, how do we find it?"

Maya straightened up, her confidence undeterred. "We dig into Eden's early files—archives, blueprints, old schematics. Somewhere in that mess is a map to this backdoor. And once we find it, we'll have a way into their system without setting off any alarms."

Jax stared at her, disbelief in his eyes. "You're talking about finding something that might not even exist anymore. And if it does, it could be locked down so tight we'll never get in."

Maya shrugged. "That's a risk we'll have to take. But I've done the research, and I'm telling you, it's our best shot. We can sit here debating all night, but the longer we wait, the more time Omnitek has to lock down their systems and come after us."

Lex ran a hand through his hair, thinking hard. Maya's plan was bold, reckless even, but it was the only lead they had. If they could find that backdoor, they could infiltrate Omnitek's core without alerting the corporation's security teams. But if they failed, the consequences would be dire.

"I'm in," Lex said finally, meeting Maya's eyes. "But we do

this carefully. We find that backdoor, and we plan out every step before we make our move. No more surprises."

Jax looked between the two of them, his expression a mix of frustration and resignation. "I don't like it. But you're right—we've come too far to back out now. Just promise me we're not going in blind."

Maya grinned, a glint of excitement in her eyes. "Don't worry. I've got a plan."

Lex stood up, feeling the weight of their decision settle over him. This was it—the next step in a fight that was quickly becoming more dangerous than any of them had anticipated. But there was no turning back now. Omnitek's control was spreading, and they were the only ones who knew enough to stop it.

As they prepared to dive back into the digital world of Eden, Lex couldn't shake the feeling that this mission would change everything. They were about to walk into the lion's den, armed only with their wits and the hope that they could outsmart the most powerful corporation on the planet.

And if they failed, there would be no second chances.

The Awakening

Lex blinked awake in his cramped apartment, his mind sluggish as the real world came back into focus. He had only unplugged from Eden a few hours earlier, but his body felt heavier, more exhausted than usual. It wasn't just the physical fatigue—it was something deeper, a lingering fog that clung to his thoughts, making it hard to shake the feeling that part of him was still in Eden.

He rubbed his eyes and swung his legs over the edge of the bed, glancing at the clock on his wall. Another night with barely any sleep. His body was sore, as if he had been running a marathon, and his fingers felt numb, stiff from hours of tapping away at the virtual controls. It didn't make sense. His real body hadn't done anything strenuous, but the strain from his time in Eden was unmistakable.

He shuffled into the small bathroom, splashing water on his face in an attempt to wake up fully. When he looked up at the mirror, he barely recognized the face staring back at him. His eyes were red-rimmed, dark circles forming underneath them, and his skin had taken on a pale, almost sickly tone.

"What the hell is happening to me?" he muttered to himself, leaning closer to the mirror. He had spent countless hours in Eden before, but this was the first time it felt like the virtual world was bleeding into his real body.

A sudden buzz from his console snapped him out of his daze. He rushed over to the screen and saw a message from Maya.

"We need to talk. Now. You feeling it too?"

Lex typed back quickly, his fingers moving slower than usual.

"Yeah. Something's wrong. Meet you at Jax's?"

"Be there in 20."

He sighed, running a hand through his disheveled hair. Whatever was happening to him, it wasn't just a result of sleep deprivation. Eden was starting to affect him in ways that shouldn't have been possible. His reflexes felt sharper, his mind more alert when he was inside the system. But outside? It was like he was falling apart.

Twenty minutes later, Lex was standing in Jax's apartment again, staring at the screens while waiting for Maya to arrive. Jax looked just as exhausted as he felt, his hands trembling slightly as he worked at his console.

"You too?" Lex asked, sitting down next to him.

Jax didn't look up, his eyes glued to the code flashing across the screen. "Yeah, man. It's getting worse. I can't tell if I'm losing it or if Eden's starting to mess with my head."

Lex leaned back in his chair, rubbing the back of his neck. "It's not just you. Something's happening. I woke up this morning feeling like I've been running for days. I've never felt this bad after a session in Eden."

Jax finally tore his eyes away from the screen, meeting Lex's gaze. "You think it's the integration? The deeper we go, the more it's... changing us?"

Before Lex could answer, Maya walked through the door, her expression grim. She dropped her bag on the floor and immediately began pacing. "It's not just physical," she said, cutting straight to the point. "It's mental too. I've been having these dreams—no, more like *memories*. But they're not mine. I'm remembering things from inside Eden, like they actually happened to me."

Lex's stomach twisted. "Memories?"

Maya nodded, her voice tense. "I'm telling you, something's happening to us. Omnitek's integration—it's pulling us deeper into Eden than we realized. Our bodies might be here, but our minds are starting to blur the lines between what's real and what's virtual."

Jax ran a hand through his hair, his expression anxious. "I thought maybe I was just imagining it. But lately, I've been reacting faster to things. Like my reflexes are improving. In Eden, it feels normal, but out here? I nearly caught a falling cup the other day without even thinking about it."

Lex leaned forward, his mind racing. "So it's not just in Eden. Whatever's happening is bleeding into the real world. Physical changes, mental changes… it's like we're evolving inside the system."

Maya stopped pacing and looked directly at Lex. "And that's exactly what Omnitek wants. Think about it—the more time we spend in Eden, the more it affects us. They've designed it that way, Lex. They're not just controlling the virtual world; they're starting to control us. Physically. Mentally. Everything."

The weight of her words hit Lex hard. It wasn't just about losing themselves to Eden anymore. Their very identities, their thoughts, their bodies were being altered by the system. And if they didn't figure out how to stop it, there might not be any turning back.

Jax broke the silence, his voice shaky. "So, what do we do? If Omnitek's figured out how to change us… do we even stand a chance?"

Lex clenched his fists, his resolve hardening. "We do. But we have to move fast. If this keeps up, we won't just lose ourselves inside Eden—we'll lose ourselves completely."

Maya nodded, her expression fierce. "We fight back. We find the source of this integration and shut it down. For good."

As the three of them sat in Jax's apartment, planning their next move, Lex couldn't shake the feeling that they were running out of time. Eden was changing them, and if they didn't stop it soon, there would be nothing left to save.

Maya leaned over the map of Eden's digital infrastructure spread across Jax's table. The glow of the multiple screens around them cast a bluish hue over the room, their faces illuminated by the constantly shifting lines of code and schematics. This wasn't the first time they had planned something big, but the stakes had never been this high. The deeper they went, the more personal it felt. Now, it wasn't just about hacking for information—it was about survival.

"We can't do this alone," Maya said, her voice steady but laced with determination. "Omnitek's reach is too vast. If we're going to take on their core systems, we need more than just the three of us."

Lex nodded, standing beside her with his arms crossed. "Agreed. We need allies. People who have seen what we've seen, who know what Omnitek is really doing inside Eden."

Jax glanced up from his console, his expression uncertain. "Yeah, but who? Most users don't even know they're being manipulated. They just think Eden is a game, a place to live out their fantasies. They're not going to care about some hidden agenda until it's too late."

Maya straightened up, her eyes hard. "There are people out

there—other hackers, underground groups who have their own reasons to distrust Omnitek. They may not know the full story, but they've seen enough to question the system. If we can get to them, show them what we've found, we might be able to rally them."

Lex stared at the map, his mind already working through the possibilities. "I know a few people who've been digging into Omnitek for years. They've stayed off the grid, but I think they'd listen if we told them what we've uncovered."

Maya nodded. "That's a start. But we need more. Jax, can you track down other users—ones who have experienced what we're going through? The glitches, the mental changes?"

Jax tapped a few commands into his console, his brow furrowing in concentration. "I can try. Omnitek's good at covering their tracks, but there are always data trails. I can search for anomalies in user behavior—people who've spent too much time in Eden, showing signs of... well, what we're dealing with."

Lex glanced at the screens as Jax worked. "It's risky. Omnitek will notice if we start tracking users that closely."

Jax didn't look up from his screen. "I know. But if we're going to take them down, we need to find others like us. We can't win this fight alone."

Maya paced the room, her mind racing. "We need to approach this carefully. We can't just start recruiting anyone. If Omnitek finds out we're building a resistance, they'll come after us before we're ready."

Lex nodded. "Right. We reach out to the ones we can trust first—other hackers, users who've been affected by the deeper integration. Once we have a core group, we can expand from there."

Jax pulled up a new screen, displaying a list of user profiles. "I've got a few leads here. These users have been showing signs of instability—sudden shifts in behavior, erratic login patterns, and extended periods of time inside Eden without logging out. I'm willing to bet they've experienced the same glitches we have."

Maya leaned over his shoulder, scanning the list. "These could be our people. But we can't just send out messages—it has to be in person, or as close as we can get in Eden. We need to make contact inside the system, feel them out before we trust them with what we know."

Lex agreed. "I'll handle that. I know how to talk to them, how to convince them we're on the same side."

Jax sighed, leaning back in his chair. "And while you do that, I'll keep digging. There's got to be more out there—other anomalies, other users who've slipped through Omnitek's grasp."

Maya stood tall, her expression fierce. "This is how we win. We build a network, underground, out of Omnitek's sight. We gather the people who can help us take them down, one step at a time."

Lex glanced at the map, then back at Maya and Jax. The plan was coming together, but they all knew the risks. Building a resistance meant exposing themselves more than ever before. If Omnitek caught wind of their movements too soon, they would shut them down before they could make a difference. But without allies, without a larger group to fight back, they stood no chance against a corporation that controlled both the virtual and real worlds.

"We'll need a base of operations inside Eden," Lex said, thinking out loud. "A place where we can meet, coordinate, and stay off Omnitek's radar."

Maya's eyes lit up with an idea. "There's an old sector in Eden, deep in the forgotten parts of the system. It hasn't been used in years—Omnitek probably doesn't even monitor it anymore. We can set up shop there, bring in recruits, and plan without them noticing."

Lex grinned. "Good. That's where we'll start."

Jax sighed again, rubbing his temples. "I can't believe we're actually doing this. A full-blown resistance? We're going up against one of the most powerful corporations in the world."

Maya placed a hand on his shoulder, her voice calm but full of conviction. "It's the only way, Jax. If we don't stop them, no one will."

As they finalized their plans and prepared to reach out to the first potential recruits, Lex couldn't help but feel the weight of what they were about to do. Building a resistance was dangerous—there was no doubt about that. But if they could gather enough people, if they could find others who were willing to fight back, they might just stand a chance.

For the first time since they had discovered the truth about Omnitek, Lex felt a flicker of hope. They weren't alone anymore. The resistance was about to begin.

The quiet hum of Eden's forgotten sector buzzed in Lex's ears as he looked over the group gathered in front of him. It wasn't much—just a handful of users, some hackers, and a few others who had experienced the strange glitches that Lex, Maya, and Jax had uncovered. But it was a start. They had managed to set up a makeshift base in this overlooked corner of Eden, a place where Omnitek's gaze didn't seem to reach, at least for now.

Lex stood at the front of the room, eyes scanning the faces of the people who had joined them. Some were hardened hackers, skilled at infiltrating systems and evading corporate surveillance. Others were users who had spent far too much time in Eden, drawn in by the perfect world Omnitek had promised, only to discover the sinister control that lay beneath the surface.

"Thanks for coming," Lex began, his voice steady but firm. He had never seen himself as a leader before, but this group needed someone to take charge. They needed direction, and he was the only one with a clear enough vision of what needed to be done. "I know most of you have heard the rumors—that Omnitek is doing more than just running Eden. You've felt it. We've all felt it. The glitches, the strange changes in our minds and bodies. It's no coincidence."

He paused, letting the words sink in. The room was silent, the group listening intently.

"What you've experienced isn't just some system bug or minor issue. Omnitek is using Eden to control us—to change us. They've built this world to manipulate our thoughts, our emotions, and even our bodies. The longer you stay in Eden, the more they're able to influence you."

A murmur rippled through the crowd. Some of them had suspected this, but hearing it confirmed out loud was different. Lex could see the fear and uncertainty in their eyes.

Maya stood beside him, her presence calm but fierce. "We've found evidence," she added, her voice strong. "Logs, files, and data that show Omnitek's been experimenting on users—changing their neural pathways, locking some people inside Eden permanently. They're taking control of everything, and if we don't stop them, they'll take over more than just the virtual world."

Lex took a deep breath, stepping forward. "We've formed

this group because we believe we can stop them. But we can't do it alone. Each of you is here because you've seen what Eden can do. You've felt it. We need people who are willing to fight back, people who know how to navigate the system, how to hack, and how to resist."

One of the hackers, a tall man with sharp eyes and a stern expression, raised a hand. "What's the plan, then? We can't just storm Omnitek's headquarters and expect to take them down. They're too powerful."

Lex nodded, acknowledging the challenge. "You're right. We can't hit them head-on, not yet. But we don't have to. Omnitek's strength is their control over the system. If we can expose that control, show people the truth, they'll start to lose their grip. We need to find the core of their operation, the source of their integration tech, and dismantle it piece by piece. Once we do that, we can weaken their hold on Eden and bring them down from the inside."

Jax, standing to the side, chimed in. "It won't be easy. Their security is airtight, and they're watching every move we make. But we've found a backdoor—a way to get into their deeper systems without triggering alarms. If we can exploit that, we'll have a shot at getting the information we need to expose them."

Another voice spoke up, this time from a young woman with bright, alert eyes. "What if they come after us? Omnitek's got enforcers, agents that can track us down in both Eden and the real world. If we're caught, it's game over."

Lex's expression hardened. "That's why we're doing this carefully. We're not going in blind. We've already set up protocols to keep our movements hidden. But we need to be smart. We only have one shot at this, and if we fail, they'll come after us with everything they've got."

He looked around the room again, seeing the determination begin to spark in some of the faces. They were scared, yes, but they were also angry—angry at Omnitek for using them, manipulating them, and trapping them in a false reality. That anger could fuel them, give them the strength they needed to fight back.

"We've already started tracking down others," Maya continued, her voice clear and direct. "People like you, who have experienced the same glitches, the same signs of Omnitek's control. The more we gather, the stronger we become. This isn't just about taking down a corporation. It's about freedom. About taking back control of our lives and our minds."

Lex stepped forward again, his eyes locking with each member of the group. "We're not just a bunch of hackers or users anymore. We're a resistance. And if we work together, we can bring Omnitek down. But we need every one of you to commit. This won't be easy. We'll be facing a corporation that's more powerful than anything we've ever dealt with. But we've got something they don't—a reason to fight."

The room fell silent again, the weight of Lex's words sinking in. Then, slowly, people began to nod. The tall hacker who had spoken earlier crossed his arms, a small grin tugging at the corner of his mouth. "Alright, Lex. I'm in. Let's see what you've got."

The others followed, one by one, agreeing to join the fight. Lex felt a surge of resolve. For the first time, he wasn't just reacting to Omnitek's actions. He was leading, and they had the beginnings of a real resistance.

As the group began to discuss logistics and next steps, Lex exchanged a glance with Maya. Her expression was unreadable, but there was a spark in her eyes that told him she believed in him. He wasn't sure how this would end, but he knew one thing for certain: they were no longer alone.

The battle against Omnitek had just begun, and Lex was ready to lead them through it.

As the newly-formed resistance huddled around the flickering digital map of Eden, Lex couldn't shake the nagging feeling gnawing at him. They were moving fast—maybe too fast. The idea of a backdoor into Omnitek's core system sounded almost too good to be true, and the deeper they delved into the corporate network, the greater the risks became.

The room was filled with hushed voices, everyone discussing plans and strategies for their next move. Jax was seated by a console, tapping away at a complex code, while Maya was running a simulation of their infiltration route. They all seemed focused, determined. But Lex couldn't ignore the tension building inside him.

Finally, Jax broke the silence with a frustrated sigh. "Lex, I've been looking over this route again. If we take that backdoor, we might get in, but there's no guarantee we'll get out clean. There's a chance we'll trip an alarm we don't even know about. Omnitek's systems are layered, and once we're in too deep… they could trap us in Eden permanently."

Lex felt the weight of Jax's words hit him like a hammer. It was the unspoken fear they had all been carrying: that Eden wasn't just a game anymore. Omnitek had built it into something more—a digital landscape where minds could be trapped, locked away from the real world.

"I know the risks," Lex replied quietly, his voice steady but tense. "But we have to keep moving forward. If we don't find out what's at the heart of Omnitek's system, they'll keep controlling people, keep trapping them inside Eden without anyone knowing."

Jax's fingers paused over the keyboard, and he turned to look at Lex, concern etched across his face. "But what if they trap *us*? We've seen what they can do. What if this is all a setup? What if that backdoor is just bait to pull us in and lock us inside for good?"

Maya stopped her simulation and turned to face the group, her expression serious. "Jax has a point. Omnitek knows how to cover its tracks. If they suspect we've found a way into their system, they could easily lay a trap for us. And once we're in too deep, there might not be a way out."

Lex stared at the digital map, his mind racing. He couldn't let fear control him, not now. But the truth was, they were entering uncharted territory. Eden wasn't just a virtual space— they were starting to realize it had the potential to reshape their minds, their very identities. And if they fell into Omnitek's hands, they might lose everything.

"Then we need a failsafe," Lex said, trying to think clearly. "We can't afford to get caught, but we also can't turn back. We need to find a way to disconnect from Eden if things go wrong— some kind of emergency exit."

Jax frowned. "That's easier said than done, man. Once you're in deep, Omnitek's got total control over your connection. If we're in the middle of their system and something goes wrong, they could lock us in. But…" He paused, rubbing his chin thoughtfully. "I might be able to rig something. A kill switch that severs our neural connection to Eden, but it's risky. If I don't calibrate it just right, we could lose chunks of our memories or worse."

Lex swallowed hard, the thought of losing memories, losing *himself* in Eden, sending a cold shiver down his spine. But they had no choice. "Do it. We need that kill switch. We're going in, but I want a way out if things get ugly."

Maya nodded in agreement. "It's the best plan we've got. But we need to be careful. Once we trigger the backdoor, we're on borrowed time. We go in, get what we need, and get out. No detours, no distractions."

The group fell into a heavy silence, the reality of the situation weighing down on them. They were on the verge of something huge—something that could bring Omnitek's entire operation crashing down. But with every step deeper into Eden, they risked losing themselves to the system. Lex knew that better than anyone.

He glanced at Jax, who was already working on the kill switch, his fingers flying over the keys with renewed urgency. The stakes were higher than ever, and Jax's tension was palpable. He had always been cautious, the one to warn them of potential risks, but even he knew that there was no turning back now.

"I'll have it ready by tomorrow," Jax muttered, not looking up from his work. "But no guarantees. This thing could either save us or fry our brains. Just so you know."

Lex managed a grim smile. "No pressure then."

Maya crossed her arms and leaned against the console, her face thoughtful. "We need to make sure everyone's on the same page. If even one person panics or breaks protocol inside, it's over. We'll be exposed, and Omnitek will have us."

Lex nodded, his mind already spinning with the weight of leadership. This was the hardest part—making sure everyone trusted each other, that no one faltered when things got dangerous. "I'll talk to the others. Make sure they understand the risks. If anyone isn't up for it, they can walk away now. No shame in it."

Maya gave him a hard look. "You think someone's going to back out?"

Lex shrugged. "Maybe. Maybe not. But I want them to know what they're getting into. We can't afford mistakes."

Maya watched him for a moment, then gave a slow nod. "You're right. No mistakes. But for what it's worth, I think they're ready. We wouldn't be here if we weren't."

Lex exhaled slowly, the weight of leadership pressing down harder than ever. He wasn't sure if he was ready to lead these people into a fight that could cost them their freedom—or their minds. But Maya was right. They were ready. He had to trust them.

As the group disbanded for the night, Lex lingered in the room, staring at the glowing map of Eden. Tomorrow, they would go deeper into Omnitek's system than they had ever gone before. And there was no guarantee they would come back the same—or come back at all.

He could feel it in his bones. This was the turning point. If they succeeded, they could dismantle Omnitek's control over Eden and free the trapped users. But if they failed… they'd be just another group of minds lost forever in the digital void.

As the lights dimmed around him, Lex made a silent promise: No matter what happened tomorrow, he would do whatever it took to protect his team. Even if it meant sacrificing himself to get them out.

Because if they were going too deep, someone had to make sure they found their way back.

The day had finally come. Lex, Maya, Jax, and a handful of trusted hackers from their fledgling resistance gathered in the shadows of Eden's forgotten sector, standing at the edge of what could be their biggest—and most dangerous—operation yet.

They were ready to exploit the backdoor Maya had uncovered, leading them into one of Omnitek's hidden virtual "factories." From what they could tell, this factory wasn't part of Eden's main experience—it was buried deep, a space where Omnitek conducted its darkest experiments, trapping users and bending their minds to its will. It was where they could find the evidence they needed to expose the corporation's manipulation of Eden and its users.

"This is it," Lex said, standing in front of the group, his tone grim but steady. "We're going in deep. This factory is where Omnitek runs its hidden programs—where they control the Deep Users and run tests on those who spend too much time in Eden. Our goal is to get in, extract the data, and get out. No detours, no heroics."

Maya nodded, her face hard with determination. "Once we're inside, we'll split into two teams. I'll lead one to find the data logs and pull everything we can. Lex will lead the other to locate the control center. We'll need to deactivate whatever security measures are keeping the system locked down."

Jax, standing off to the side, looked more nervous than usual. He had the kill switch ready, as promised, but the tension in the room was thick. They all knew the risks. If anything went wrong, they could be trapped in Omnitek's system permanently.

"Everyone clear?" Lex asked, scanning the group. They all nodded, though he could see the flicker of fear in their eyes. This was no ordinary hack. They were stepping into the belly of the beast.

"Alright," Lex continued. "Let's move."

The team connected to Eden, and the world around them

shifted. In an instant, they left the safety of the forgotten sector and found themselves standing in front of a towering, ominous structure—a factory unlike anything they had seen in the public-facing parts of Eden. The walls were a dull, metallic gray, and strange sounds hummed from deep within. The air felt thick, almost oppressive, like the digital space itself was designed to crush those who entered.

"Stay sharp," Maya said, her voice tense. "This place isn't like the rest of Eden. They don't expect regular users to find it, which means security will be tight."

Lex led the group toward a heavy, rusted door at the base of the factory. As Jax worked on disabling the entry lock, Lex couldn't shake the eerie feeling that something was watching them. Omnitek had been quiet lately—too quiet. He knew it was only a matter of time before they made a move.

With a soft click, the door opened, revealing a long, dimly lit corridor that stretched into the heart of the factory. They entered cautiously, their footsteps echoing off the metal walls. The deeper they went, the more Lex felt like they were descending into something unnatural, something that wasn't supposed to exist in Eden.

"This place is wrong," one of the hackers muttered under their breath.

Maya shot them a warning glance. "Focus. We're here to get the data, not to freak out."

They continued down the corridor until they reached a large central chamber, filled with strange machinery and screens displaying endless streams of data. Dozens of cables snaked across the floor, leading to pods that were lined up in neat rows along the walls. Each pod contained a user, their bodies still, their eyes locked in a blank, unseeing stare. Lex's stomach turned as he realized what they were looking at.

"These are the Deep Users," Maya whispered, her voice low with horror. "They're trapped here, their minds plugged into Eden, but their bodies…"

Lex stepped forward, staring at the pods. "They're using them. Keeping them in Eden while their real bodies waste away in the physical world. This is how Omnitek controls them."

Jax, visibly shaken, ran his hand through his hair. "This is insane. We knew they were experimenting on people, but this… this is worse than we thought."

"We need to get the data and get out," Lex said, forcing himself to stay focused. "Maya, take your team and start downloading everything you can from the logs. We need hard proof of what they're doing here."

Maya nodded, quickly leading her group toward the rows of consoles lining the far wall. They worked quickly, their fingers flying over the digital interfaces as they began extracting files. Meanwhile, Lex led his team toward the control center, where they could disable any active security systems and keep the place from going into lockdown once Omnitek realized they were inside.

"Jax, how's it looking?" Lex asked as they reached the main control hub.

Jax was already typing furiously, pulling up layers of security protocols. "It's bad. Their system is woven into everything here. If we trip an alarm, the whole place will lock down, and we'll be trapped."

"Can you stop it?" Lex asked, his eyes scanning the room for any signs of trouble.

Jax nodded, though his voice was tense. "Yeah, but it's going to take time. Just keep watch while I work."

As Jax worked to disable the security, Lex kept an eye on the surroundings. The room was eerily quiet, save for the soft hum of machinery. His mind raced, thinking of the people trapped in the pods—innocent users who had come to Eden for escape, only to become prisoners of Omnitek's hidden agenda.

Suddenly, a sharp beep cut through the air. Lex's heart dropped as Jax's face went pale.

"What is it?" Lex asked, his voice low.

"We've got a problem," Jax muttered. "I just tripped an alert. They know we're here."

Before Lex could respond, the factory around them seemed to come alive. The dim lights flickered, and the hum of the machines grew louder. On the screens, warning messages flashed, and Lex could hear the faint sound of footsteps—Omnitek's enforcers, closing in.

"Maya, we're compromised!" Lex shouted into the comm. "Get your team out now! We're about to be overrun."

"We're almost done!" Maya's voice came through, laced with urgency. "Give us one more minute."

"We don't have a minute!" Lex snapped. He turned to Jax, who was frantically working to shut down the incoming security forces. "Jax, get that kill switch ready. We're not getting out of here clean."

Jax's hands moved faster, the pressure mounting as the sound of approaching enforcers grew louder. "It's ready," he said through gritted teeth. "But if we use it now, we'll lose half the data Maya's team is pulling."

"We'll take what we can get," Lex growled. "Get ready to pull us out."

In the chaos, Lex's mind raced. They had come so far, only to risk losing everything at the last second. But he couldn't afford to let anyone get trapped here—not today, not ever.

"Now, Jax!" Lex shouted as the doors to the control room burst open.

In an instant, everything went black.

Reality is Broken

The world came back into focus slowly, like waking from a bad dream. Lex gasped for breath as he ripped the neural visor from his head, feeling the cold sweat drip down the back of his neck. His apartment's dim lights seemed blinding after the darkness of Eden's factory, and for a moment, he wasn't sure where he was.

"Lex, you alright?" Jax's voice crackled through the comms.

Lex blinked, trying to steady his racing heart. His hands were still trembling as the reality of what had just happened set in. "Yeah," he muttered, his voice hoarse. "I'm here. Barely."

Around him, the small apartment felt even more claustrophobic than usual, the walls seeming to close in as his mind struggled to process the near-disaster they had just escaped. Maya's voice cut through the haze.

"We got out, but it was close," she said, her tone as sharp as ever. "Too close."

Lex glanced at the screen in front of him. The factory had been a nightmare, and they had barely managed to extract any data before Jax had triggered the kill switch. The enforcers had been closing in, and if they had stayed even a second longer, they wouldn't have made it out.

"How much data did we get?" Lex asked, trying to shift his

focus.

Maya was silent for a moment, clearly running calculations. "Not as much as we hoped. Maybe half of what we were pulling, if we're lucky."

Lex clenched his fists. They needed more—much more—to expose Omnitek's full operation. But at least they had something. Proof of the Deep Users, of Omnitek's twisted experiments. It wasn't a complete victory, but it was a step.

Jax's voice broke the silence, frustration clear in his tone. "We can't go back to that sector anytime soon. They'll have locked it down tight now. We need to figure out our next move."

Lex rubbed his temples, trying to calm the storm of thoughts swirling in his mind. They had survived, but Omnitek knew they were coming for them now. The corporation wasn't going to sit back and let them expose everything. They would retaliate, and next time, there might not be a way out.

"I know," Lex said quietly. "We're not safe. We need to lay low for a while, regroup. If Omnitek knows we're after them, they'll come after us."

Maya didn't sound happy, but she agreed. "We'll have to change locations. Omnitek has eyes everywhere, and we're exposed now. We can't afford to be predictable."

Jax chimed in, his voice more cautious. "We're also running out of time. You've felt it, right? The changes, the glitches. Every time we go into Eden, it feels… different. Like the system is wrapping itself around us."

Lex didn't need to be reminded. His own body felt like it was still half in Eden, like the world around him was nothing more than a shadow. Ever since they had started pushing deeper into Omnitek's systems, reality had begun to blur at the edges. He could feel the virtual world creeping into his thoughts, affecting him in ways he couldn't quite explain.

"I've noticed it too," Lex admitted, his voice low. "It's like we're getting pulled deeper every time we log in. It's not just the glitches anymore—it's the way the virtual and the real are starting to merge. If we're not careful, we're going to lose track of what's real."

Maya let out a long sigh. "That's Omnitek's goal, isn't it? They want us to lose ourselves in Eden. They want everyone to."

Lex nodded, though no one could see him. "And that's why we need to stop them. But first, we need to disappear for a while. We need to find a new base, somewhere they can't track us."

Jax grunted in agreement. "I'll start looking for another spot in Eden where we can regroup. Somewhere off the grid, like the old sector. But it's going to take time."

Lex leaned back in his chair, staring up at the ceiling, his mind still racing. The mission had been close, too close. They had narrowly escaped Omnitek's grasp, but the fight was far from over. If anything, it was just beginning. Omnitek had resources they couldn't even fathom, and now they knew that Lex and his group were coming for them.

"Okay," Lex said finally. "We go dark. Jax, find us a new spot. Maya, comb through the data we got—see if there's anything we can use. We need to hit Omnitek harder next time. No more close calls."

"Got it," Maya said, her voice resolute. "We'll be ready."

As the comms fell silent, Lex sat alone in the quiet of his apartment, the weight of their mission pressing down on him. They had escaped Omnitek's grasp this time, but they wouldn't get so lucky again. If they were going to take down the corporation, they had to be smarter, faster, and more prepared than ever.

And deep down, Lex knew that the deeper they went into Eden, the harder it would be to come back out.

The days that followed the failed hack were tense. The resistance had gone dark, moving carefully through Eden and avoiding any major actions while Jax searched for a new base. But the cracks in the group's unity were starting to show.

Lex could feel it, a growing tension between them. Maya was focused, pushing harder than ever to analyze the data they'd pulled from the factory. She barely slept, and when she did, it was fitful. Jax, on the other hand, had become more distant, his usual confidence giving way to doubt. He'd always been the cautious one, but now it seemed like fear was starting to take root.

It wasn't long before the tension finally boiled over.

They had gathered in Maya's small apartment, their usual meeting place when they needed to be off-grid in the real world. The air was thick with frustration, and Lex could feel the weight of their failure pressing down on him.

"We need to move faster," Maya said, pacing the room, her voice sharp. "Omnitek's tightening their grip, and we're sitting here doing nothing."

Jax, seated at the small table, glanced up at her, his expression dark. "Nothing? You think I'm doing nothing? I've been working non-stop to find us a safe place to regroup. I'm the one keeping us off Omnitek's radar. Meanwhile, you're running simulations and analyzing data like we have all the time in the world."

Maya stopped pacing and glared at him. "We *don't* have time, Jax. That's exactly the point. The deeper we go into Eden, the more we're changing. I've seen it in myself, and I know you've felt it too. Omnitek is turning Eden into a trap, and if we don't stop them soon, we'll all be too far gone to do anything about it."

Jax threw his hands up, frustration written all over his face. "You think I don't know that? Every time I go into Eden, I feel like I'm losing pieces of myself. But running headlong into Omnitek's systems without a plan is suicide, Maya. You saw what happened last time. We barely made it out alive!"

Lex watched them both, his jaw clenched. The argument wasn't new, but it was getting worse. They were both right in their own ways. Maya was pushing them to act before Omnitek could close in, but Jax was right about the risks. One wrong move, and they'd all end up trapped in Eden, just like the Deep Users they were trying to save.

"Enough," Lex said, stepping forward, his voice firm but controlled. "We can't afford to be fighting each other. Omnitek's the enemy, not us."

Maya's eyes flashed with anger, but she forced herself to take a breath, her hands resting on the back of a chair. "I'm not trying to fight, Lex. I'm just saying we need to take more action. We can't let fear paralyze us."

Jax crossed his arms, his voice low. "Fear is what's keeping us alive right now. I'm not saying we stop, but we have to be smart about this. Every time we log in, we're playing with fire."

Lex stood between them, feeling the weight of their words pressing on him. He knew they were both right, and that was what made this so hard. They couldn't afford to wait too long, but rushing in without a plan would be fatal. They needed to strike a balance, and it was his job to find it.

"We need a new approach," Lex said after a long pause. "Jax, keep working on finding us a safe spot. We'll need somewhere secure if things go sideways again. Maya, keep digging through the data. If there's anything we can use against Omnitek, I want to know about it. But until we're ready, we lay low. No unnecessary risks."

Maya looked like she wanted to argue, but after a moment, she sighed and nodded. "Fine. But we can't sit on our hands forever, Lex. The longer we wait, the more time Omnitek has to tighten its grip."

"I know," Lex said, his voice calm but resolute. "But we're not just hacking into some corporate server anymore. We're going after the heart of Eden. If we rush this, we lose everything."

Jax leaned back in his chair, his expression softening just a bit. "I'm not trying to drag us down, Lex. I just don't want us to get in over our heads. Omnitek's already one step ahead of us. If we're going to win this, we need to be smart."

Lex nodded. "And we will be. But we can't fall apart now. We're too close."

The room fell into a tense silence, the weight of their situation hanging over them like a storm cloud. They were fighting for more than just their own survival—they were fighting for the minds and lives of everyone trapped in Omnitek's web. But with each passing day, it felt like the corporation's grip was tightening, and Lex couldn't shake the feeling that their time was running out.

"Let's regroup tomorrow," Lex said finally, breaking the silence. "We'll make a plan, but we'll do it right. No more rushing in without thinking it through."

Maya gave him a tight nod, though he could see the frustration still simmering beneath the surface. Jax didn't say anything, but Lex could tell the tension between them hadn't been fully resolved.

As the group dispersed, Lex sat alone for a moment, the quiet of the room pressing in on him. The cracks in the group were small now, but if they didn't find a way to hold together, they would break completely—and Omnitek would win.

He knew he had to keep them united, but he also knew the pressure was mounting. Every day, Omnitek was one step closer to finding them, one step closer to trapping them in Eden forever.

As he stared at the empty room, Lex made a silent vow to himself: No matter what it took, he would find a way to pull his team back together. Because if they couldn't trust each other, they didn't stand a chance against Omnitek.

And time was running out.

Lex sat in the darkened room, his eyes locked on the streams of data flowing across the screen. Maya had sent over another file—one of the fragments they'd managed to extract from the factory. It was different from the rest. Most of the data they'd pulled was detailed logs of users, manipulation programs, and Omnitek's tracking systems. But this? This was something else entirely.

The lines of code twisted and shifted in ways Lex had never seen before. It wasn't just raw data; it was almost... alive. He leaned closer, his fingers hovering over the keyboard, hesitant to dive in but too curious to stop himself.

He started breaking it down, isolating parts of the code, looking for patterns. The more he examined it, the stranger it became. Unlike the standard corporate coding used by Omnitek, this looked like a hybrid—a mix of regular programming and something deeper, something embedded at a level even Lex wasn't familiar with.

"What are you hiding?" he muttered to himself, his mind

racing.

Hours passed as he delved deeper into the data. It wasn't just a hidden file—it was more than that. This code was linked to Eden's very core, connected to the architecture that powered the entire virtual world. But it wasn't just operating Eden. It was *changing* it.

Lex's heart pounded as he realized what he was looking at. This code was designed to rewrite Eden itself, to bend reality within the system. It wasn't just controlling users—it was warping the entire environment. The system wasn't simply a platform Omnitek used to manipulate people's emotions or thoughts. It was evolving, reshaping itself in response to the users inside.

He quickly pulled up his comms and connected to Maya. Her face flickered onto the screen, tired but alert. "What's up, Lex? You find something?"

"You need to see this," Lex said, his voice urgent. "That file you sent me from the factory—it's not just data. It's something more. It's a *control script*."

Maya frowned, clearly confused. "What do you mean, control script? Like a monitoring tool?"

"No," Lex shook his head, his fingers moving rapidly across the keyboard as he shared his screen with her. "It's a script that rewrites Eden itself. It's not just manipulating the users. It's warping the entire environment, bending reality inside the system. It's evolving."

Maya's eyes widened as she watched the lines of code scroll past. "This isn't possible," she muttered, leaning in closer to her screen. "Are you saying Eden's... *alive?*"

"Not alive," Lex replied, his voice tight. "But it's adapting. This code is reacting to the users inside. It's rewriting the very foundation of the virtual world, responding to their thoughts, their emotions. And the deeper we go, the more it's changing us."

Maya leaned back, her face pale. "This is bigger than we thought. If Omnitek has found a way to let Eden evolve, it explains everything—the glitches, the physical changes we've been experiencing. The system isn't just affecting us. It's learning from us. It's building itself around our minds."

Lex stared at the code, his mind racing. "It's why the boundaries between Eden and reality are starting to blur. It's not just that we're spending too much time inside the system. The system is shaping itself around us. The longer we're connected, the more it molds to our thoughts, our fears, our desires."

Maya was silent for a moment, processing the gravity of what Lex was saying. "So Omnitek isn't just controlling people. They're controlling *reality* inside Eden. They've built a system that adapts to the users and keeps them locked in, without them even realizing it."

Lex nodded, his voice tight. "And the worst part? It's not just virtual. It's starting to leak into the real world. You've seen it, right? The way we've been feeling when we log out. It's like we're still connected. Our minds aren't just in Eden when we're logged in—they're *staying* there, even after we disconnect."

Maya cursed under her breath. "Omnitek's been hiding this the whole time. They're using us to refine the system, to perfect this… this *evolving* trap."

"We need to shut it down," Lex said, his resolve hardening. "This isn't just about freeing the Deep Users anymore. If we don't stop this, Eden will completely consume anyone who stays in too long. They'll lose themselves completely, and it won't just be their minds. It'll be their *reality*."

Maya's face was grim, but there was a fire in her eyes. "We can use this, Lex. If we can expose what Omnitek is doing—if we can show people that Eden is warping reality itself—they won't be able to hide it anymore. But we need to find where this code is coming from, where it's being executed. It's not just running on a regular server."

"I know," Lex said, already thinking through the next steps. "It's coming from deep inside Omnitek's core. We'll need to go farther than we've ever gone before. The last time we barely made it out. This time… it could be worse."

Maya didn't hesitate. "We have to take the risk. If we don't, Omnitek will keep refining this system until no one can tell what's real and what's not. We need to find the heart of Eden and rip this code out before it spreads."

Lex nodded, his mind already working on the plan. He knew it would be dangerous, but there was no other choice. The system was growing, evolving into something beyond their control. If they didn't act now, they might lose everything.

"Alright," Lex said, his voice filled with determination. "We're going in. And this time, we're going to take Eden apart."

As he closed the connection with Maya, Lex felt a strange sense of clarity wash over him. The lines between Eden and reality were blurring, but this time, he knew what was at stake. They weren't just fighting for control over a virtual world—they were fighting for control over their very minds.

And they were running out of time.

The plan was in motion. Lex, Maya, Jax, and a few others from their growing resistance stood at the edge of Eden's virtual underbelly—a part of the system that had been abandoned for years, where the old code from Eden's earliest versions still lingered. This was where Omnitek's core control was hidden. The evolving code they had discovered was connected to this place, and if they could find the source, they could expose Omnitek and finally shut it down.

But there was one problem they hadn't anticipated.

As the group moved deeper into the digital landscape, Lex's screen flickered. The space around them was filled with glitches—faint, ghostly images that faded in and out of existence. The deeper they went, the more unstable the environment became, as if Eden itself was warping around them, reacting to their presence. Jax's face was pale, his hands trembling slightly on his keyboard.

"This place is a mess," Jax muttered. "It's like the system's tearing itself apart."

Maya, leading the way, glanced over her shoulder. "It's not falling apart. It's *reacting* to us. The evolving code is in play."

Lex's gut twisted as he pushed forward. They were getting close—he could feel it—but the unease in the pit of his stomach wasn't just about the glitching environment. Something else was wrong, something that had been nagging at him since they started this mission.

Suddenly, a figure materialized in front of them, emerging from the shadows as if pulled from the very code of Eden itself. The avatar was tall, clad in sleek, black armor that shimmered with the same glitches that surrounded them. Its face was obscured by a dark visor, and a glowing emblem of Omnitek pulsed on its chest.

The group froze. Lex's heart pounded as he instinctively stepped forward, trying to shield Maya and Jax. He had heard rumors about this figure but had never encountered it directly: Omnitek's top agent, known only as "Specter." He was a ghost in the system, a shadow that appeared when Omnitek needed to deal with threats personally.

"Lex," Specter said, his voice smooth and unsettling, a digital distortion that sent chills down Lex's spine. "I knew it was only a matter of time before you made your move."

Lex clenched his fists, his mind racing. He hadn't expected Omnitek to send its enforcer after them so soon. Specter was more than just a high-level agent—he was rumored to be directly connected to Eden's core, a living weapon Omnitek used to eliminate anyone who got too close to the truth.

"What do you want, Specter?" Lex said, his voice steady despite the tension in the air.

Specter tilted his head slightly, as if amused. "What do I want? To stop you, of course. You and your little resistance have caused enough trouble. You should have known Omnitek would never let you get this far."

Maya stepped forward, her eyes blazing with defiance. "You're just another puppet for Omnitek. You think you're powerful, but you're as much a prisoner as the rest of the users trapped in Eden."

Specter's visor flickered for a moment, the light behind it shifting in an almost imperceptible way. "You think you know what's going on here, don't you? But you're wrong. Omnitek isn't the enemy. Eden is the future—this is the evolution of humanity. The longer you fight it, the more you doom yourselves."

Lex's jaw tightened. "You're wrong. Eden isn't about freedom. It's about control. Omnitek wants to own us, body and mind. We're here to stop that."

Specter let out a low, distorted chuckle. "Stop it? You don't understand, do you? You can't stop Eden. It's already too late.

The code you've been digging into—the code you think you can destroy—it's part of something bigger. Something you can't even comprehend."

The words hit Lex like a punch to the gut. He had always known there was more to Eden than they had uncovered, but Specter's cryptic tone suggested something even worse than he had imagined. His mind raced, trying to find a way to deal with Specter, but the truth was sinking in. They were in over their heads.

Before Lex could respond, Specter raised his hand, and the environment around them began to shift. The glitches intensified, and suddenly the walls of the virtual space started closing in, the code warping and twisting around them like a trap.

"You've wasted enough of my time," Specter said, his voice cold. "I'll make this quick."

Maya reacted first. "Lex, we need to move—now!"

Lex's instincts kicked in. "Jax, get us an exit route!"

Jax was already scrambling, his fingers flying across the keyboard. "I'm trying! Specter's locking down the whole sector. I can't get us out without tripping Omnitek's security protocols."

The walls of code continued to close in, and Specter advanced on them, moving with a terrifying calm. He wasn't in a hurry—he knew he had them trapped. Lex's heart raced. This wasn't just another enforcer. Specter was toying with them, and he had no intention of letting them escape.

"Lex, we can't fight him head-on!" Maya shouted, her eyes darting between Specter and the collapsing environment.

"I know!" Lex shouted back, his mind racing. "We need to split up. It's the only way."

Maya hesitated, but she knew Lex was right. If they stayed together, Specter would cut them down one by one. But if they split up, they had a chance—however slim—of getting out.

"Alright," she said, her voice tight. "But you better make it out of here."

Lex gave her a tight nod. "Jax, trigger the diversion program we set up last week. It's our only shot."

Jax's fingers flew across the keyboard, and the environment around them flickered again, this time with a purposeful distortion. For a moment, the digital landscape fractured, creating multiple copies of the group, as if they were glitching in and out of existence. It was enough to confuse Specter, just for a second.

"Go!" Lex yelled.

Maya and Jax bolted in opposite directions, their avatars splitting off as the glitches intensified. Lex stayed behind for a moment, watching as Specter paused, clearly trying to assess the situation.

Specter's visor flared, and his voice dripped with amusement. "Clever. But you can't run forever."

With that, Specter vanished into the shadows, his presence evaporating like smoke in the wind. Lex didn't wait. He turned and ran, his heart pounding in his chest. They had bought themselves a little time, but Specter wasn't done with them. He would find them again, and next time, there might not be an escape.

As he sprinted through the glitching corridors of Eden's broken sector, Lex's mind raced. Specter's words echoed in his head—*You can't stop Eden.* But Lex knew one thing for sure: he wouldn't stop fighting. Even if Eden was evolving, even if Specter was right about the power Omnitek wielded, they couldn't let it win.

Because if they did, there would be nothing left of reality at all.

Lex sprinted through the chaotic digital corridors of Eden, his heart pounding in his chest. The glitching walls warped and twisted around him, a constant reminder of how close they were to losing control of everything. Specter's words echoed in his mind—*You can't stop Eden*—but Lex wasn't ready to accept that. Not yet.

As he ran, his comms crackled to life. It was Maya, her voice sharp with urgency.

"Lex, we've lost Jax's signal. He's gone dark."

Lex's stomach dropped. "What? Where was he last?"

"I don't know!" Maya's voice was strained. "The moment we split up, Specter must have gone after him. I can't get a lock on his location, and I've got enforcers closing in on my end."

Lex's mind raced. They had planned for tight situations, but not like this. The plan to split up had been a desperate move, and now they were paying the price. Jax was their tech lead, the one who kept them connected and safe inside Eden. If Specter had caught him, they were in more trouble than Lex wanted to admit.

"Keep moving, Maya," Lex said, his voice tense. "I'll find Jax."

"Be careful, Lex," Maya warned. "Specter's still out there, and he's hunting us. Don't try to be a hero."

Lex disconnected the call, his focus shifting entirely to Jax. His friend had been quiet for too long, and that wasn't a good sign. Navigating through Eden's increasingly unstable environment, Lex pulled up the last known location of Jax's signal. It was deep within the sector, near the core of the factory they had infiltrated.

The corridors grew darker and more fragmented as Lex approached the area. The walls flickered with static, bending in unnatural ways as Eden's evolving code continued to distort reality. It felt like he was moving through a dream—or a nightmare—where nothing was quite solid, and every step could lead to a trap.

Then, Lex saw him.

Jax was standing in the middle of a large chamber, his avatar flickering and distorted, a clear sign that he had been compromised. Specter was there too, looming over him like a shadow. The sleek, dark figure of Omnitek's top agent was perfectly still, as if waiting for Lex to arrive.

"Let him go!" Lex shouted, stepping forward, his fists clenched.

Specter didn't turn to face him immediately. Instead, he tilted his head slightly, the smooth, distorted voice dripping with cold amusement. "You should have stayed hidden, Lex. This was never your fight to win."

Lex stepped closer, his eyes locked on Jax, who was barely conscious, his body trembling under the weight of the code Specter had used to trap him. "Jax," Lex called out, his voice shaking slightly. "Can you hear me?"

Jax looked up weakly, his voice a faint whisper. "Lex... it's bad. He's got me... locked in."

Lex's mind raced, trying to figure out a way to save him. But Specter was too close, too powerful. Every second they stayed here was a second closer to total defeat.

"You can't save him," Specter said, his voice cold and certain. "He's already part of Eden now. Just like you will be."

Lex took another step forward, his heart pounding. "No. I won't let that happen."

He could feel the weight of the moment pressing down on him. He had two choices: he could try to fight Specter head-on, which would almost certainly end in failure, or he could do something else—something far more dangerous.

Jax's voice came through the comms again, weak but determined. "Lex… listen to me. You need to go. You can still escape, but I can't. Specter's already locked me in. If you stay, we both go down."

"No," Lex said firmly, his voice cracking. "I'm not leaving you here."

"You don't have a choice," Jax replied, coughing slightly. "I can feel it, Lex. I'm too deep in the system. Specter's got me tied to Eden's core. But… there's one way I can help. I can shut down this part of the system. It'll give you and Maya enough time to get out, but it'll trap me here for good."

Lex's heart clenched. "No. I'm not letting you sacrifice yourself. We'll find another way."

"There is no other way," Jax said, his voice soft but resolute. "You need to stop Omnitek, Lex. And this is the only way I can help you do that."

Specter remained silent, watching the exchange with a detached amusement, as if he already knew the outcome.

Lex's mind raced, but deep down, he knew Jax was right. They were out of time, and if Jax could give them even a few more minutes to escape, it might be enough to save them both. But the thought of leaving his friend behind, trapped inside this twisted version of Eden, was almost unbearable.

"Jax," Lex whispered, his voice breaking. "I can't…"

Jax managed a faint smile. "You have to. This is the only play we've got. Tell Maya… tell her I'm sorry."

Lex's hands trembled as he stepped back, his heart pounding.

"I'll stop them, Jax. I swear. I'll stop Omnitek, and I'll come back for you."

Jax's smile faded as the weight of his decision settled over him. "Good luck, Lex. Get out of here."

Before Lex could say another word, Jax's avatar flickered, and then the entire chamber began to shake. Specter moved to intervene, but it was too late—Jax had activated the failsafe. The walls of code around them began to collapse, folding in on themselves as the system started to shut down.

"Go!" Jax shouted, his voice echoing through the collapsing environment.

Lex turned and ran, his heart pounding in his chest. As he sprinted through the glitching corridors, the sound of Specter's distorted laughter followed him. But Lex didn't stop. He couldn't.

Behind him, the sector began to implode, disappearing into the black void of Eden's collapsing code. Jax had made the ultimate sacrifice to give them a chance, and now it was up to Lex to make sure it wasn't in vain.

He burst out of the collapsing sector, barely making it to the exit as the walls behind him dissolved into nothingness. Maya's voice came through the comms, panic in her tone.

"Lex? Are you out?"

"I'm out," Lex said, his breath ragged. "But Jax... Jax didn't make it."

There was a long silence on the other end.

"Did he...?" Maya's voice broke slightly.

"He saved us," Lex replied quietly. "He gave us the time we needed."

As the digital landscape of Eden stabilized around him, Lex clenched his fists, the weight of Jax's sacrifice settling over him like a crushing burden. Specter was still out there, and Omnitek was more dangerous than ever.

But now, this was personal.

"I'm going to finish this, Maya," Lex said, his voice filled with a quiet fury. "I'm going to take Omnitek down. For Jax."

Maya's voice was filled with a mixture of sorrow and determination. "For Jax."

And with that, Lex disconnected the comms, his resolve hardening.

This wasn't just about stopping Omnitek anymore. It was about vengeance, about justice for the friends he had lost. And no matter what it took, he would tear Eden apart to get it.

Omnitek had won a battle, but the war was far from over.

Battle of Realities

Lex sat in the corner of the dimly lit room, staring blankly at the wall. The usual sounds of the city outside—the distant hum of traffic, the occasional siren—barely registered in his mind. His body was in the real world, but his thoughts were trapped somewhere else, somewhere between Eden and reality. He hadn't felt truly present since the moment Jax sacrificed himself. It was like a part of him had been left behind in Eden, and no matter how hard he tried, he couldn't fully disconnect.

His hands still shook from time to time, as if they were searching for the controls that weren't there. His vision blurred occasionally, as if the real world was glitching, just like Eden. It was as though the line between the two worlds was fading, and he couldn't tell where one ended and the other began.

Maya's voice snapped him out of his daze.

"Lex?" she asked, sitting down beside him, her eyes filled with concern. "You haven't said much since… since we got out."

Lex blinked, trying to focus. He hadn't realized how long he had been sitting there, lost in his thoughts. "I'm fine," he said quietly, though he knew that wasn't true.

Maya frowned, clearly not convinced. "We're not fine, Lex. None of us are. Eden is affecting us in ways we never expected.

It's more than just a game now—it's starting to bleed into the real world. You've felt it too, haven't you?"

Lex nodded, the weight of her words sinking in. He had felt it, and not just in the way his mind seemed to drift between realities. His body felt different too. His reflexes were sharper, his senses more attuned, as if Eden had changed him on a fundamental level. But there were side effects too—like the fatigue that never left him, the headaches that seemed to come and go, and the dreams... the dreams that felt more like memories of a place he was never supposed to stay.

"It's like my mind is still in Eden," Lex said softly, his voice barely above a whisper. "Even when I'm awake, I feel like I'm still connected."

Maya nodded. "I've been feeling it too. The longer we stayed in, the more real it became. And now that we're out, it feels like Eden hasn't fully let us go. It's not just a system anymore, Lex. It's something else, something alive. And it's holding on to us."

Lex's chest tightened as he listened to her. Maya was right. Eden was no longer just a virtual world. It had evolved, and Omnitek had designed it to blur the boundaries between the digital and the physical. But it wasn't just about control anymore—Eden was becoming something more, something that could reach into the real world and warp it.

"I don't know what to do," Lex admitted, his voice shaking slightly. "Every time I close my eyes, I see it. I feel like I'm losing myself. Like I'm becoming a part of Eden, even when I'm not logged in."

Maya reached out and grabbed his hand, squeezing it tightly. "You're not losing yourself, Lex. We're still here, still in control. But we need to figure this out, fast. Whatever Omnitek is doing, it's getting worse. And if we don't stop it soon, Eden might not just be a place we visit—it could become our reality."

Lex nodded, though his mind was still clouded with uncertainty. He knew she was right, but the thought of going back into Eden, of confronting Specter again, of facing the truth about what they were becoming—it terrified him.

Just then, the door to the room creaked open, and one of the resistance members stepped in, his face pale. "Lex, Maya, you need to see this."

Lex exchanged a worried glance with Maya before following the man into the next room. There, in front of a wall of screens, the rest of their group was gathered, their faces filled with dread.

On the screens, multiple news feeds were playing, each showing footage of strange phenomena occurring all over the city. Buildings were flickering, just like the glitches they had seen inside Eden. People were collapsing in the streets, clutching their heads as if they were in pain. Others were staring at their hands, watching in horror as they seemed to fade in and out of reality, just like avatars glitching in the virtual world.

Lex's stomach dropped as he took it all in. The line between Eden and the real world wasn't just blurring—it was breaking down entirely.

"Omnitek's integration has spread," the man who had called them in said, his voice tight with fear. "It's not just happening inside Eden anymore. Whatever they've done, it's leaking into the real world. People are losing their grip on reality, and it's getting worse by the hour."

Lex felt his hands start to shake again. This was exactly what they had feared—Eden wasn't just a virtual trap anymore. It was rewriting reality itself, and it wasn't stopping.

"We have to shut it down," Maya said, her voice firm. "Now. If we don't, there won't be anything left to save."

"But how?" another member of the group asked. "Omnitek controls everything. They've got the entire system on lockdown, and even if we could get back inside Eden, we don't know where the core is."

Lex stared at the screens, his mind racing. The images of the flickering world outside, of people trapped between two realities, filled him with a deep sense of dread. He could feel Eden pulling at him again, as if it were calling him back.

"We find the source," Lex said quietly, his voice filled with determination. "We find where Omnitek is running the evolving code, and we shut it down. For good."

Maya looked at him, her eyes filled with both fear and hope. "It's going to be dangerous, Lex. We might not make it out this time."

Lex nodded, his jaw set. "I know. But we don't have a choice. If we don't stop it now, Eden will become the only reality there is. And that's not a world I'm willing to live in."

The group fell silent as Lex's words sank in. They all knew what was at stake, and they all knew that this would be the hardest fight they had ever faced. But Lex could see it in their eyes—the same determination he felt. They weren't just fighting for their own survival anymore. They were fighting for the future of the world.

"Let's get to work," Lex said, stepping forward, the weight of the coming battle heavy on his shoulders.

As they began preparing for the mission, Lex felt the pull of Eden stronger than ever. The virtual world had broken through the walls of reality, and now it was up to him and his team to stop it before it consumed them all.

There was no turning back now. The battle between the real and the virtual had begun, and only one would survive.

The room was filled with the low hum of tech equipment as Lex, Maya, and the rest of the resistance gathered around the large, makeshift table. The tension in the air was palpable. Everyone knew what they were about to attempt could be the last thing they ever did. But it didn't matter. They were past the point of hesitation.

Maya stood at the head of the table, her face illuminated by the flickering glow of several monitors displaying maps, code, and detailed schematics of Eden's core systems. The evolving code, now corrupting both Eden and the physical world, had to be stopped at the source. It was their only chance.

"So," Maya began, her voice cutting through the silence, "we've found the source of the evolving code. It's buried deep in Omnitek's mainframe, hidden in a section of Eden we've never accessed before. But here's the problem: it's fortified, protected by multiple layers of encryption and security systems we've never seen."

Lex leaned forward, his eyes scanning the map on the screen. The target location, a sector simply labeled **Origin**, was marked deep inside Eden, farther than they had ever gone before. The word itself sent a shiver down his spine. This was it. The heart of Eden. The place where it all began.

"That's where it's being controlled from," Maya continued. "The evolving code is tethered to the Origin. If we can breach it, we can shut it down and sever Omnitek's control over both Eden and the real world."

Jax's absence was still fresh, and the weight of what had happened to him hung over them like a shadow. Lex could almost hear Jax's voice echoing in his head, warning them about the dangers of diving too deep. But now, they had no choice. Jax had sacrificed himself to give them a shot at stopping this, and Lex wasn't about to let that sacrifice be in vain.

One of the resistance members, a hacker named Vex, raised her hand. "What about Specter? You know he's going to be guarding the core. There's no way Omnitek's top agent lets us waltz into their most secure system without a fight."

Lex exhaled sharply. She was right. Specter had been a constant threat, and now that they were aiming for the heart of Omnitek's control, he'd be waiting for them. But this time, Lex was prepared. He had been thinking about Specter ever since their last encounter, replaying it over and over in his mind.

"We can't avoid Specter," Lex said, his voice firm. "But I've studied him. He's connected directly to the system, and that's his strength—but it's also his weakness. Specter relies on the system to give him power, and if we disrupt the flow of code in the Origin, we can weaken him long enough to take him down."

Maya raised an eyebrow. "You think we can take him down?"

Lex nodded. "We have to. He's not just an enforcer. He's part of the evolving code. If we don't stop him, we won't stand a chance at getting to the core."

There was a moment of silence as the group absorbed Lex's words. The risks were enormous, but there was no other option. They had seen what was happening to the world outside—Eden was bleeding into reality, and soon there wouldn't be anything left to fight for.

Vex tapped a few commands into her terminal, pulling up a more detailed schematic of the Origin sector. "Okay, I've analyzed the security layers. The first few levels are the usual stuff—encryption, firewalls, AI guards—but once we get closer to the core, it gets… weird. The code starts shifting, like it's rewriting itself in real-time."

"It's the evolving code," Maya said, her voice grim. "It's protecting itself. The closer we get, the more it'll change to stop us."

Lex stood, staring at the map. "Then we don't give it time to adapt. We move fast. In and out before it knows what's happening."

"But that means we'll be vulnerable," Vex warned. "We won't have time to set up defensive measures."

Lex clenched his fists. "I know. But if we don't shut this down, none of us will survive—inside Eden or outside."

Maya stepped up beside Lex, placing a hand on his shoulder. "We can do this, Lex. We've come too far to stop now."

Lex looked around the room, meeting the eyes of each member of the resistance. They were scared, and they had every reason to be. But they were also determined. This wasn't just about stopping Omnitek anymore. It was about saving the world from being rewritten into something unrecognizable.

"Alright," Lex said, his voice steady. "Here's the plan. We're going in with two teams. Maya and I will lead the first team into the Origin. We'll be the ones to shut down the core. Vex, you lead the second team and handle the security layers. We need you to clear the path and disrupt any defenses that might slow us down."

Vex nodded, her fingers already working to adjust the parameters on her terminal. "Got it. I'll have my team working through the encryption layers in real-time. Just don't take too long—once we start, Omnitek's going to know we're coming."

"We won't take longer than we have to," Lex promised. "But be ready to pull us out if things go sideways."

Maya shot him a look. "We're not pulling out, Lex. Not this

time."

Lex hesitated for a moment but then nodded. She was right. They were all in now. There was no turning back.

As they continued to finalize the plan, the weight of what was ahead pressed down on them. This mission wasn't like the others. They were going straight into the heart of Omnitek's system, into a place where the lines between the virtual and real worlds no longer mattered. If they failed, Eden would consume everything—and there wouldn't be a second chance.

The team broke apart, preparing their gear, running simulations, and making final adjustments to the encryption keys they would need to bypass the layers of security. Lex watched them work, feeling the gravity of the moment settle over him like a heavy cloak.

Maya walked over to him, her expression serious. "Are you ready for this?"

Lex took a deep breath, his mind flashing back to everything they had been through—their early days as hackers, the resistance they had built, Jax's sacrifice. It had all led them to this moment.

"I don't know if I'll ever be ready," Lex admitted quietly. "But we have to do it anyway."

Maya gave him a small, encouraging smile. "That's all that matters."

As the final preparations were made, Lex stood tall, the weight of leadership heavy on his shoulders but his resolve unshakable. He knew what was at stake, and he knew they couldn't afford to fail.

The world was breaking apart around them, and if they didn't stop Omnitek and shut down the evolving code, there wouldn't be anything left to save.

"Let's move out," Lex said, his voice steady but filled with the fire of determination.

The final battle was about to begin.

The plan was set, and there was no turning back. Lex, Maya, and the rest of the team stood at the edge of Eden, staring into the abyss of the sector known as the Origin. The swirling, shifting code surrounding the entrance was like nothing they had seen before. It pulsed with energy, constantly evolving and changing, just like the glitching reality outside. The deeper they went, the more dangerous it would become, and they all knew it.

Lex clenched his fists, his heart pounding. Every nerve in his body screamed that this was a bad idea, but he forced the fear down. This was the only way to stop Omnitek and save the world from being rewritten by Eden's evolving code.

"Ready?" Maya asked quietly, standing beside him. Her voice was calm, but Lex could see the tension in her eyes.

"Ready as I'll ever be," Lex muttered, pulling up the holographic interface of his gear, making last-minute checks. "Let's do this."

With a deep breath, the team stepped forward, crossing the threshold into the Origin. As soon as they did, the environment around them shifted. The digital landscape became surreal, almost dreamlike. The ground beneath their feet shimmered and glowed, and the air felt thick, like they were moving through water. It was as if Eden itself was alive, watching them.

"Keep moving," Lex ordered, trying to keep his voice steady. "We're on a timer."

Behind them, Vex and her team began working on the first layer of encryption, their fingers flying across the virtual keyboards as they cracked through Omnitek's security. The entrance to the Origin was heavily guarded by complex algorithms and AI constructs that shifted and adapted to every move they made.

"Layer one's almost down," Vex reported, her voice crackling through the comms. "We've got AI guardians tracking us, but we're keeping them busy. Just get to the core as fast as you can."

"Understood," Maya replied. "We'll push forward."

The deeper they went, the more unstable the environment became. Glitches appeared in the walls, flickering images of the real world leaking into Eden. Lex could see brief flashes of people outside—citizens collapsing in the streets, buildings shimmering like holograms as the boundary between Eden and reality continued to break down.

Maya's face was tense as she watched the glitches. "It's getting worse. We don't have much time before the real world starts falling apart completely."

"I know," Lex said through gritted teeth. "We need to move faster."

They reached the first checkpoint—a massive, glowing gate made of shifting code. It twisted and reformed with every passing second, its defense mechanisms adapting to any potential threats. This was one of the barriers protecting the Origin, and they needed to breach it to get closer to the core.

"Vex, we're at the gate. Can you shut it down?" Lex asked.

Vex's voice came through, laced with concentration. "Give me a minute. This thing's adapting fast, but we're almost through the second encryption layer."

Maya glanced around, her eyes sharp. "Specter's going to show up soon. He's not going to let us get this close without intervening."

Lex nodded, feeling the weight of her words. Specter was out there, watching, waiting for the right moment to strike. But they didn't have a choice. They had to keep going, no matter the cost.

Suddenly, the gate flickered, and a path opened before them. "Gate's down!" Vex shouted. "But I've got a lot of incoming heat—AI units are locking onto our position. You don't have long."

"Go!" Lex ordered.

They moved quickly, stepping through the gate and into the next sector. The landscape beyond was even stranger—massive pillars of glowing code stretched up into the sky, twisting and pulsing like the veins of a living organism. The entire space felt alive, as if it was watching them, adjusting to their presence.

"We're getting close to the core," Maya said, her eyes scanning the horizon. "This is the heart of Eden. It's where the evolving code is being generated."

Lex felt a chill run down his spine. They were entering the most dangerous part of Omnitek's system, the place where reality itself was being rewritten. The code here was raw, constantly shifting and adapting, and if they weren't careful, it could consume them.

"Stay sharp," Lex warned. "Anything could happen here."

They moved cautiously, weaving through the shifting landscape as they approached the final barrier. This was it—the last defense between them and the core of Eden. Lex could feel the energy in the air, the code thrumming with power as it responded to their presence. It was as if the system knew they were coming, and it was ready to fight back.

Just as they reached the final gate, the air around them shifted. A familiar presence appeared in the distance, a figure materializing out of the shimmering code.

Specter.

Lex's heart skipped a beat as the dark figure approached, his sleek, armored form shimmering with the same glitches that surrounded them. His visor glowed with an eerie light, and his voice, cold and distorted, echoed through the space.

"You should have stayed away, Lex," Specter said, his voice dripping with menace. "This is beyond you. Eden is evolving, and you can't stop it."

Lex stepped forward, his jaw clenched. "I don't care how powerful you think Eden is. We're going to shut it down."

Specter tilted his head, his movements unnaturally smooth. "You don't understand. Eden is no longer just a virtual world. It's becoming something more—something that will reshape reality itself. And you… you're standing in the way of progress."

Maya raised her weapon, her voice steady. "This isn't progress. This is control. And we're here to stop you."

Specter laughed, a cold, metallic sound that sent chills through Lex's spine. "You're too late. Even if you reach the core, Eden will continue to evolve. It's already rewriting the world outside. You can't stop what's already begun."

Lex didn't respond. He knew there was no reasoning with Specter. Omnitek had turned him into a weapon, and now he was nothing more than a tool to defend the system.

"Vex," Lex said, his voice tight. "Shut the gate down. We'll hold Specter off."

"Working on it!" Vex replied, her voice strained. "But this last layer is a nightmare. I need a few more minutes."

"We don't have a few minutes," Maya muttered, her eyes locked on Specter.

Specter moved toward them, his form glitching in and out

of existence as the system around him shifted. He was faster, stronger than anything they had faced before, and Lex knew that defeating him would take everything they had.

"Lex," Maya said quietly, her voice filled with determination. "I'll keep him busy. You focus on getting to the core."

Lex's heart tightened. "Maya, you can't take him on alone."

"I'm not planning on winning," she said, her eyes fierce. "I just need to buy you enough time."

Before Lex could respond, Maya charged forward, her weapon drawn as she met Specter head-on. The two clashed in a flurry of motion, their movements a blur as they fought through the shifting code.

Lex felt a surge of panic, but he forced himself to focus. He couldn't afford to lose control now. Maya knew the risks, and she was willing to make the sacrifice.

"Come on, Vex," Lex muttered under his breath. "We need that gate down."

"Almost there," Vex replied, her voice tense. "Just hold on a little longer."

Lex watched as Maya fought Specter, her movements swift and precise. But Specter was relentless, his attacks powerful and unyielding. Lex knew she couldn't hold him off forever.

Finally, Vex's voice came through the comms, filled with relief. "Gate's down! You're clear!"

Lex's heart raced. This was it.

"Maya!" Lex shouted. "The gate's open!"

Maya turned, her eyes locking with Lex's for a brief moment. Then, with a final burst of energy, she pushed Specter back and sprinted toward the gate.

Specter recovered quickly, his visor glowing with fury as he chased after them.

"Go!" Lex shouted.

They sprinted through the gate, the core of Eden just ahead of them.

This was their chance.

They had to stop the evolving code.

Before it consumed everything.

Lex and Maya burst through the gate into the heart of Eden, the core of the evolving code. The landscape before them was unlike anything they had ever seen—an endless, shifting expanse of raw data, glowing with an eerie, pulsating light. Tendrils of code wove through the air like living organisms, constantly shifting and reforming as they moved. This was the Origin, the place where Omnitek had created Eden, and now the source of its terrifying evolution.

Maya stopped for a moment, breathing hard as she took in the surreal sight. "This is it," she whispered. "The heart of Eden."

Lex stared at the pulsing, chaotic center of the core, feeling a strange pull toward it. It was almost hypnotic, like the system itself was calling out to him, trying to lure him closer. He shook his head, forcing himself to focus. They didn't have time to hesitate. The evolving code was still rewriting both Eden and the real world, and if they didn't shut it down now, it would spread beyond their control.

"We need to move fast," Lex said, his voice tight. "Specter's right behind us."

Maya nodded, her face set with determination. "I'll hold him off for as long as I can. You need to access the core and shut it down."

Lex opened his mouth to argue, but Maya cut him off with a sharp look. "This isn't up for debate, Lex. You're the only one who can break into the core. You've studied this code more than anyone else. I'll buy you the time you need."

Lex clenched his fists, knowing she was right but hating the thought of leaving her to face Specter alone again. He wanted to protect her, to fight beside her, but he also knew that if they didn't stop the evolving code, none of them would make it out alive.

"Be careful," he said, his voice low.

Maya gave him a grim smile. "I always am."

Without another word, she turned and sprinted back toward the entrance, where Specter was closing in fast. Lex watched her go, his heart tightening with fear. But he couldn't afford to think about that now. He had a job to do.

Turning back to the core, Lex accessed his interface, pulling up the encrypted protocols that protected the heart of Eden. The code here was dense, layered with complex firewalls and adaptive defenses that shifted constantly. He'd never seen anything like it—it was as if the system was alive, anticipating his every move.

He started working, his fingers flying over the virtual keys as he bypassed the first layer of security. The evolving code fought back, trying to block his access, but Lex had spent years learning the intricacies of Eden's architecture. He knew how to navigate its defenses, even if they were now shifting in ways he hadn't anticipated.

The deeper he went, the more the core resisted. It was like trying to wrestle with a living thing, each piece of code reacting to his attempts to break through. Lex gritted his teeth, pushing forward, his focus razor-sharp.

Outside, he could hear the sounds of Maya and Specter clashing, their battle echoing through the air. Maya's determined grunts and Specter's cold, distorted laughter reverberated through the environment. Lex tried to shut it out, forcing himself to stay focused.

He broke through the second layer of security, then the third. He was getting closer, but the core was fighting harder now. The code around him twisted and surged, trying to push him back, trying to corrupt his access.

"I'm almost there," Lex muttered to himself, sweat beading on his forehead.

Suddenly, his comms crackled to life. It was Vex. "Lex, we're losing control of the security layers! Specter's forces are overwhelming us! We don't have much time!"

Lex's heart pounded in his chest. He knew time was running out, but he couldn't rush this. One wrong move, and the system could lock him out completely—or worse, trap him inside Eden for good.

"I'm working on it," he replied, his voice tight with concentration. "Just hold on a little longer."

Vex didn't respond, but Lex could feel the pressure building. He couldn't let them down—not after everything they'd been through. Not after Jax.

He broke through the final layer of encryption, reaching the core of Eden. It was a massive, glowing sphere of pure, shifting data. The code surrounding it pulsed with energy, and Lex could feel the immense power it held. This was the source of the evolving code, the heart of everything Omnitek had created.

Lex hesitated for a brief moment, overwhelmed by the sheer magnitude of what he was about to do. This wasn't just a system—they were standing in the very heart of Eden's creation, the place where the virtual world had been born and where it had begun to evolve into something far more dangerous.

Taking a deep breath, Lex reached out and began inputting the override commands. He had prepared for this moment, spent countless hours studying the core's structure, knowing that one day he might need to shut it down. But now that he was here, with the fate of the world hanging in the balance, it felt more real than ever.

As he input the final sequence, the core started to react. The pulsing lights dimmed, the tendrils of code slowing their frantic movements. Lex's heart raced as he realized it was working—the core was shutting down, the evolving code losing its grip.

"Lex," Maya's voice came through the comms, strained and breathless. "Hurry. Specter's…"

Her voice cut out, replaced by a burst of static.

"Maya!" Lex shouted, panic surging through him. But there was no response. He was alone in the core, the sounds of the battle outside now eerily silent.

With a final, desperate push, Lex entered the last command, and the core went dark. The glowing sphere flickered and dimmed, and the tendrils of code fell limp, collapsing into nothingness. The evolving code was defeated.

But the victory felt hollow as Lex stood there, staring at the lifeless core. Maya's voice was gone, and the silence weighed heavy on him.

He turned and sprinted back toward the entrance, his heart pounding in his chest. As he neared the spot where Maya had fought Specter, his worst fears were confirmed.

Maya lay on the ground, motionless, her avatar flickering weakly as the environment around them stabilized. Specter was gone, but the damage had been done.

Lex dropped to his knees beside her, his hands shaking. "Maya," he whispered, his voice hoarse. "Maya, come on. We did it. We shut it down. You can't leave me now."

Her eyes flickered open for a moment, and she managed a weak smile. "You... you did it," she whispered, her voice barely audible. "You stopped it."

Lex shook his head, tears stinging his eyes. "We stopped it. We did this together."

Maya's smile faded, her avatar glitching again. "Lex... I don't think I'm coming out of this."

"No," Lex said firmly, his voice breaking. "Don't say that. We're getting out of here, together."

But deep down, he knew. The damage was done, and Maya wasn't going to make it. Specter had fought too hard, and the evolving code had taken too much.

"Promise me," Maya whispered, her voice fading. "Promise me you'll finish this. Don't let them rebuild Eden. Don't let Omnitek win."

Lex swallowed hard, his heart breaking. "I promise."

With one last, faint smile, Maya's avatar flickered one final time and then disappeared, her form dissolving into the digital ether.

Lex knelt there, staring at the empty space where she had been, the weight of the loss crushing him. He had shut down the evolving code, but the cost had been too high.

The battle for Eden was over, but Lex knew the fight wasn't finished. Omnitek would try again, and it was up to him to make sure they never succeeded.

As he stood up, his fists clenched, Lex made a vow. He had lost Jax. He had lost Maya. But he wouldn't let their sacrifices be in vain.

Omnitek had created Eden. Now, he would tear it down.

Lex sat alone in the cold, dim glow of his apartment. The

once-familiar hum of the city outside felt distant, muted, as if the world had moved on without him. Everything felt different now—both the physical world and Eden. They had stopped the evolving code, but the cost had been unimaginable. Jax, Maya… they were gone. The fight had ended, but the war inside Lex raged on.

He stared at the neural visor lying on the table in front of him. The thin, sleek device had once been his gateway into Eden, into a world of endless possibilities, a world where he could escape the dreariness of reality. Now, it was a symbol of everything he had lost. He hated it. He wanted to smash it, to throw it across the room and destroy it for good.

But he couldn't.

Because the truth was, even with Omnitek's evolving code shut down, Eden still existed. The virtual world was still there, still calling out to him, a siren song of control and deception. And more importantly, Omnitek still existed. The corporation might have suffered a blow, but they weren't defeated. Lex knew they would try again—maybe not today, maybe not tomorrow, but eventually. Eden was too valuable, too powerful for them to abandon.

As much as Lex wanted to walk away, to leave it all behind and forget the digital nightmare that had cost him his friends, he knew he couldn't. Maya's last words echoed in his mind: *Promise me you'll finish this. Don't let them rebuild Eden.*

Lex sighed, leaning forward and burying his face in his hands. He felt like a ghost, drifting between two worlds—one real, one virtual—and belonging to neither. He had spent so much time inside Eden, so much time fighting to free people from its grasp, that he didn't know how to live in the real world anymore. Every time he closed his eyes, he could still see it—

the glowing, pulsing core of Eden, the tendrils of code reaching out like they were alive.

He didn't know what was real and what wasn't anymore.

The door to his apartment creaked open, and Lex looked up, startled. Vex stood in the doorway, her face somber but determined. She had been one of the few who had survived the final push into the Origin, and though they had both made it out alive, neither of them had walked away unscathed.

"How are you holding up?" Vex asked, stepping inside and closing the door behind her.

Lex shrugged, his voice flat. "I'm still here. That's about all I can say."

Vex nodded, pulling up a chair and sitting across from him. "I know how you feel. It doesn't seem real, does it? We fought so hard, but it's like the world outside hasn't even noticed."

Lex stared out the window, watching the distant lights of the city. "Omnitek controls everything. Most people don't even know what we did. They'll keep living their lives, plugging into Eden like nothing happened."

Vex leaned forward, her expression hardening. "Maybe. But we stopped them, Lex. You stopped them. Without the evolving code, Eden isn't the same. It's still there, but Omnitek can't control people the way they did before. You made a difference."

Lex shook his head, bitterness rising in his throat. "It doesn't feel like enough. Maya and Jax are gone, and for what? Eden is still standing. Omnitek is still out there."

"But it's weaker now," Vex said firmly. "They lost control of their most powerful weapon. You exposed them. And the people who know the truth? They're not going to let Omnitek get away with it again. You're not alone in this."

Lex looked down at the neural visor, his reflection distorted in the smooth surface. "I promised Maya I'd finish it," he said quietly. "But I don't even know what that means anymore."

Vex was silent for a moment, then she reached across the table and placed a hand on Lex's arm. "You've done enough, Lex. You don't have to carry this alone. We'll find a way to bring Omnitek down for good, but you don't have to destroy yourself in the process."

Lex stared at her hand, feeling a strange sense of comfort in her words. He had been so focused on the fight, so consumed by the need to stop Omnitek, that he had forgotten what it meant to live outside of that battle. He had been ready to give everything, even his own life, but now, with Jax and Maya gone, he wasn't sure he had anything left to give.

"Maybe you're right," Lex said softly. "Maybe it's time to let someone else take the lead."

Vex smiled faintly, her eyes filled with understanding. "You've earned that, Lex. But when the time comes, when Omnitek tries again, we'll be ready. And we'll finish what we started."

Lex nodded, feeling a weight lift off his shoulders. For the first time in what felt like years, he allowed himself to breathe, to really breathe. He didn't have to carry the burden of Eden alone anymore. There were others—people like Vex—who believed in the same fight. And even though the pain of losing his friends would never fade, he knew that their sacrifices hadn't been in vain.

As Vex stood to leave, Lex picked up the neural visor, turning it over in his hands. He wasn't ready to go back into Eden. Not yet. But one day, he knew he would. One day, he would face Omnitek again and finish what they had started.

"Vex," Lex said as she reached the door.

She turned, raising an eyebrow. "Yeah?"

"Thanks," Lex said quietly, his voice filled with gratitude.

Rebuilding the Resistance

It had been weeks since the collapse of the evolving code, and Lex had finally started to emerge from the haze that had clouded his mind. The weight of Jax and Maya's deaths still hung heavy over him, but the urgency of the mission had kept him moving. There was no time for rest, no time to truly grieve—not yet.

Lex stood at the entrance of an old, abandoned warehouse on the outskirts of the city. The air was cold, and the sky was an ominous shade of gray, but the inside of the warehouse buzzed with activity. This was where the next phase of their fight would begin. The warehouse had become the new base for the resistance, a place where they could operate off-grid and rebuild their forces without Omnitek watching their every move.

As he stepped inside, Lex was greeted by the sounds of keyboards clicking, low voices exchanging ideas, and the hum of various tech devices being repaired and upgraded. The resistance was small, but it was growing again, attracting hackers, rogue developers, and those who had seen firsthand the dangers of Omnitek's grip on Eden. They were all here for the same reason: to finish what Lex, Maya, and Jax had started.

Vex was already inside, standing in front of a large digital map projected on the wall, discussing logistics with a few other key members of the group. She looked up as Lex approached, her expression one of quiet determination.

"How's it looking?" Lex asked, his voice steady, though fatigue still lingered in his bones.

Vex crossed her arms and nodded toward the map. "We're making progress. We've got teams working on new security protocols, hacking into Omnitek's lower-level systems, trying to track their movements. They're being quiet for now, but we know they're planning something."

Lex glanced at the map, which displayed a network of glowing lines—Omnitek's digital infrastructure. He knew they couldn't trust the silence. Omnitek might have lost control of the evolving code, but they hadn't disappeared. The corporation was regrouping, and Lex was certain they would try again to reclaim Eden, to perfect the system that had nearly consumed the world.

"They're waiting for the right moment," Lex said, his voice low. "They're not done with Eden. They'll come back stronger, more prepared."

Vex sighed, brushing a strand of hair from her face. "That's what we're preparing for. We need to be ready when they strike. We need to hit them before they get the chance to rebuild."

Lex leaned against a nearby table, watching the people around them work. The atmosphere was tense but determined. The new recruits were focused, determined to bring down Omnitek once and for all. But Lex couldn't help but feel a pang of doubt. Could they really win this war? Could they truly take on a corporation as powerful as Omnitek and survive?

"How many new recruits?" Lex asked, his voice quieter now, almost to himself.

Vex turned to him, her expression softening. She knew what was on his mind. "We've got about thirty, maybe more coming in next week. Small teams, but they're skilled. They know what we're up against."

Lex nodded, though the doubt lingered. Thirty people. It wasn't much against the might of Omnitek, a company that had billions in resources and some of the most advanced technology in the world. But then again, they had never had the numbers on their side. Their strength had always been in their ability to move quickly, to hit where Omnitek wasn't expecting.

"We need more than just hackers," Lex said after a moment. "We need allies on the outside—people who can expose Omnitek for what they really are. If we keep fighting them from the shadows, we'll never bring them down completely."

Vex smiled slightly, her eyes gleaming with that familiar fire Lex had come to rely on. "I've been thinking about that too. We have contacts in the media, some whistleblowers who are ready to come forward. If we can get the right evidence, we can blow Omnitek's operations wide open. But it's risky. They'll come after anyone who tries to expose them."

"Let them come," Lex said firmly. "We're not running anymore."

Vex nodded, and for a moment, they stood in silence, watching the rest of the team work. It was a strange feeling—being back in the fight, knowing that every step they took brought them closer to another clash with Omnitek. But this time, Lex felt different. He wasn't just reacting anymore. He wasn't just trying to survive. He was ready to take the fight to them, to make them pay for everything they had done.

"Lex," Vex said softly, breaking the silence. "I know things haven't been easy since… since we lost Jax and Maya. But you've got to remember why we're doing this. We're not just fighting to take down Omnitek. We're fighting for a future where no one has to live in fear of being controlled. That's what they wanted."

Lex looked down at his hands, the weight of her words settling over him. She was right. Jax and Maya hadn't given their lives just to stop Omnitek. They had fought for a world where people could choose their own path, where they weren't prisoners in a virtual prison. And now, it was up to him to make sure their vision became a reality.

"I know," Lex said quietly. "I won't forget."

Vex placed a hand on his shoulder, her expression softening. "You're not alone in this, Lex. We're all with you. We'll make sure Omnitek never rebuilds Eden the way they planned."

Lex met her gaze, and for the first time in a long while, he felt a sense of hope. They had lost so much, but they weren't finished. The fight wasn't over, and as long as they stood together, they still had a chance to win.

"Alright," Lex said, standing straighter, his resolve returning. "Let's get to work. We've got a corporation to bring down."

Vex grinned and nodded. "That's the Lex I remember."

As they turned back to the map and began discussing their next moves, Lex felt a renewed sense of purpose. He knew the road ahead wouldn't be easy—Omnitek was still out there, still dangerous—but for the first time in weeks, he felt like they had a real shot.

They were rebuilding the resistance, stronger than ever. And this time, they wouldn't stop until Omnitek was finished for good.

Lex would make sure of it.

For Jax. For Maya.

And for the future they had all fought so hard to protect.

The days that followed were a blur of activity. The resistance was growing, but Lex knew they couldn't take on Omnitek alone. They needed allies—people who could help them fight this battle on multiple fronts. As Lex stood in the heart of the warehouse, watching the teams work on new strategies and monitoring Omnitek's movements, he knew that their next step would be crucial. They had to expand beyond the underground, reach out to people in positions of influence, and find those willing to expose Omnitek for what it was.

Vex joined him at a nearby table, a data pad in hand. "I've been thinking about your idea," she said, pulling up a list of contacts. "We need to bring in people who can do more than just hack into systems. We need journalists, politicians, anyone with a platform. If we can get them to speak out, Omnitek won't be able to hide in the shadows anymore."

Lex nodded, his mind already racing through possibilities. "Who do we have so far?"

Vex handed him the data pad, where a list of potential allies scrolled across the screen. Some were investigative reporters with a history of taking down corrupt corporations. Others were whistleblowers, former Omnitek employees who had seen the dark side of the company's operations but had been too afraid to come forward. A few were politicians, mostly on the fringes of the political world, but influential enough to make waves if they had the right evidence.

"We've got a few names, but none of them are going to jump in without something concrete," Vex explained. "They know Omnitek's dangerous. They've seen the influence the corporation has over the media and the government. If they're going to risk their careers—or their lives—they need undeniable proof."

Lex exhaled sharply. "We've got some data from the last mission, but it's not enough. We need something bigger, something that proves Omnitek's direct involvement in manipulating Eden and its users."

Vex leaned back, thinking for a moment. "There's a man I've been tracking—Alexander Kane. He's a former Omnitek executive, someone who was deep inside their operations before he left. No one knows why he disappeared, but rumor has it he's been hiding out somewhere off-grid. If we can find him, he might have the proof we need."

Lex frowned, his mind turning over the name. He'd heard it before—a shadowy figure whispered about in the hacking community. Kane had vanished almost two years ago, and there had been no sign of him since. If they could track him down, though, it could be the break they needed.

"Where do we start looking?" Lex asked.

Vex pulled up a map, zooming in on a location near the city's industrial district. "He's been spotted here, in a place called The Fringe. It's a rundown part of the city, mostly inhabited by people who want nothing to do with the grid. It's a dangerous place, but if anyone knows where Kane is, it's the people hiding out there."

Lex studied the map, noting the areas marked as high-risk zones. "It's a long shot, but it's worth it. If we can get Kane to talk, it could change everything."

Vex nodded. "We'll need to be careful. The Fringe is crawling with mercenaries, bounty hunters, and Omnitek agents looking for people exactly like him."

Lex looked up from the map, his eyes narrowing. "Then we go quietly. We can't let Omnitek know we're looking for Kane.

If they find him first, he's as good as dead."

Later that night, Lex and Vex made their way toward the outskirts of the city, heading into The Fringe. The air here was different—thicker, more oppressive, like the weight of the city's neglect had settled into the very atmosphere. The streets were narrow and winding, with crumbling buildings on either side, their windows dark and broken. Few people wandered the streets, and those who did kept their heads down, avoiding eye contact.

"This place feels like it's barely hanging on," Vex muttered, her eyes scanning the alleys for any sign of trouble.

Lex nodded. "That's why people like Kane hide here. Omnitek wouldn't waste resources on this place unless they knew he was here."

They moved quietly, keeping to the shadows as they navigated deeper into the district. Vex had arranged a meeting with a local contact, someone who might know where Kane was hiding. As they approached a dingy, half-collapsed warehouse, Lex's instincts kicked in. Something about the area felt off—too quiet, too empty. He motioned for Vex to stay close.

Inside the warehouse, they were greeted by a man who looked like he had spent too many years hiding from the world. His clothes were ragged, his face lined with worry and exhaustion. He was their contact, a former hacker named Rook, who had disappeared from the grid years ago.

"You looking for Kane?" Rook asked, his voice rough, eyes darting nervously around the room. "You're not the first."

Lex stepped forward, keeping his voice low. "We don't have time for games. If you know where he is, tell us."

Rook hesitated, wringing his hands together. "He's been laying low, but I've heard whispers. He's nearby, but Omnitek's got people sniffing around. If you're looking for him, you need to get to him before they do."

Vex leaned in. "Where is he?"

Rook glanced around, his paranoia palpable. "There's an old tech facility on the edge of the district. Abandoned years ago. That's where he's been seen."

Lex nodded, but before he could thank Rook, there was a sudden movement at the far end of the warehouse. The door slammed open, and several armed figures stormed inside, their faces hidden beneath masks.

"Go!" Lex shouted, pulling Vex toward a side exit.

They sprinted through the maze of alleyways, the sound of footsteps pounding behind them. Mercenaries. They had been made.

"Omnitek's already here," Vex growled as they ducked into a narrow alley, catching their breath. "They must have heard we were looking for Kane."

"We have to find him before they do," Lex said, glancing around the corner to check if they were still being followed. "We can't lose him."

They moved quickly, sticking to the shadows and avoiding the main streets. Lex's heart raced as they neared the old tech facility. If Kane was here, they would have to get him out fast—before Omnitek's agents could lock down the area.

As they approached the building, Lex spotted movement inside. A figure stood near the back, rummaging through old, discarded equipment. It was him. It had to be.

"Kane!" Lex called out, moving toward him.

The figure froze, turning to face them. It was Alexander Kane, though he looked different than Lex had imagined—older, more haggard, like a man who had seen too much. His eyes were sharp, though, and there was no mistaking the intensity in his gaze.

"Who are you?" Kane asked, his voice wary, as if expecting a trap.

"We're here to help," Lex said quickly. "We know who you are, and we need your help to bring down Omnitek. They're coming for you. We need to move."

Kane's eyes narrowed, but before he could respond, the sound of footsteps echoed through the building. The mercenaries had found them.

"Too late," Vex muttered, pulling out her weapon. "We're going to have to fight our way out."

Lex tightened his grip on his own weapon, turning to Kane. "We need to get you out of here. Now."

Kane nodded, his expression grim. "Lead the way."

With the mercenaries closing in, they had no choice but to fight their way out. But now, they had Kane—and with him, the key to taking down Omnitek for good.

The sound of footsteps echoed off the walls of the abandoned tech facility, growing louder by the second. Lex's heart raced as he, Vex, and Kane pressed themselves against a corner, trying to stay out of sight. The mercenaries were closing in fast, their dark silhouettes cutting through the shadows.

"How many are there?" Vex whispered, her eyes scanning the room as she gripped her weapon tightly.

"Too many," Lex muttered, his mind racing. They were boxed in, surrounded on all sides, and they had no idea how much longer they could stay hidden. "We need to get out of here before they find us. Kane, do you know any exits?"

Kane, his face etched with lines of worry and exhaustion, glanced around. "There's a service tunnel that runs beneath the building. It's old, but it should get us out of here."

Lex nodded, relief washing over him. "Show us."

Kane led them to a rusted, half-hidden door at the far end of the facility. It was barely noticeable among the debris and disrepair, and Lex realized it was likely how Kane had managed to avoid detection for so long. As Kane pushed the door open, the tunnel stretched out in front of them, dark and foreboding, but it was their only chance.

"Go," Lex urged, motioning for Kane to move first. "Vex and I will cover you."

Kane didn't need to be told twice. He slipped into the tunnel, disappearing into the darkness, while Vex and Lex stood by the entrance, weapons at the ready. The mercenaries were getting closer, their voices now audible through the thin walls of the building.

"We don't have much time," Vex whispered, her voice tight with urgency.

Lex nodded. "Let's move."

They darted into the tunnel, pulling the door shut behind them just as the first mercenary entered the room. The tunnel was narrow and cramped, but it was their only path to safety. The air inside was damp and stale, the faint sound of dripping water echoing in the distance. As they moved through the darkness, Lex kept his hand on his weapon, ready for anything.

Kane led the way, his steps sure despite the unfamiliar terrain. Lex couldn't help but admire the man's resilience. Kane had been in hiding for years, constantly looking over his shoulder, yet he still moved with the confidence of someone who knew what was at stake.

"How much farther?" Vex asked, glancing back to ensure they weren't being followed.

"Not far," Kane replied. "There's a ladder up ahead that leads to the surface, but we'll have to be quick. They'll figure out we're down here soon enough."

As they reached the ladder, Lex paused, listening. The faint sounds of the mercenaries were distant now, but he knew it wouldn't stay that way for long. They needed to get out, and fast.

"You go up first," Lex said to Kane. "Vex and I will follow."

Kane nodded and began climbing, his movements slow but steady. Vex waited for him to clear the top before she started her ascent, her sharp eyes still scanning the tunnel for any sign of danger.

Lex followed last, keeping his weapon drawn as he ascended. The ladder led to a rusty metal grate that opened onto a back alley. The moment they were out, Lex felt the cool night air hit his face, a stark contrast to the stale, suffocating air of the tunnel. They were outside, but not yet safe.

Vex glanced around the alley, checking for any signs of the mercenaries. "We're clear, for now."

Kane leaned against a wall, catching his breath. "I know somewhere we can lay low," he said, his voice hoarse. "There's an old safehouse a few blocks from here. Omnitek doesn't know about it. We'll be safe there."

Lex wasn't sure how much he trusted Kane yet, but they didn't have many options. He nodded, signaling for Kane to lead the way.

The streets were mostly empty as they moved through the city, sticking to the shadows and avoiding the main roads. The tension in the air was palpable, every noise making Lex's heart race as he expected to see Omnitek's mercenaries around every corner. But the night was eerily quiet, almost too quiet.

After what felt like an eternity, they arrived at the safehouse—a small, unassuming building tucked between two larger warehouses. The door was reinforced, but Kane opened it with a keycard that seemed too advanced for such a rundown area. Inside, the space was sparse but functional, filled with outdated tech equipment and a few basic supplies.

"We'll be safe here," Kane said, collapsing into a chair and running a hand through his disheveled hair. "At least for now."

Vex immediately moved to check the perimeter, making sure there were no tracking devices or signals that could give away their location. Meanwhile, Lex turned to Kane, his mind racing with questions.

"We need to know everything you know about Omnitek," Lex said, his voice low but firm. "You were an executive. You have access to information that could bring them down."

Kane nodded, though his eyes were heavy with exhaustion. "I'll tell you everything, but you need to understand something—what Omnitek is doing with Eden is bigger than you think. The evolving code you stopped? That was just one piece of their plan."

Lex's heart sank. He had suspected that Omnitek's ambitions went beyond the evolving code, but hearing it confirmed was like a punch to the gut. "What are they planning?"

Kane leaned forward, his voice dropping to a near-whisper. "They're not just trying to control Eden. They're trying to merge it with reality. The evolving code was a test, an experiment to see how far they could push the boundaries between the virtual world and the real one. But now that it's been stopped, they're going to accelerate their plans. They're going to try again, and next time, it'll be bigger."

Lex's blood ran cold. The idea of Omnitek merging Eden

with reality, creating a world where people could no longer tell the difference between the two, was terrifying. It would give the corporation absolute control over both worlds, and there would be no escaping it.

"How do we stop them?" Lex asked, his voice filled with urgency.

Kane looked up at Lex, his expression grim. "There's a place—a hidden facility where Omnitek is developing the technology to merge the two realities. It's heavily guarded, and no one outside the highest levels of the company knows where it is. But I do. I helped build it."

Vex reentered the room, her face pale. "Omnitek is watching the streets. We don't have much time before they figure out where we are."

Lex turned to Kane. "We need to hit that facility before they finish their work. If we can destroy it, we can stop Omnitek's plans for good."

Kane nodded slowly. "I'll take you there. But it won't be easy. If we're going to stop them, we're going to need more than just a small team of hackers. We're going to need an army."

Lex felt the weight of his words settle over him like a heavy cloak. The fight wasn't over—far from it. But now, they had a chance. They had Kane, they had the location of Omnitek's facility, and they had the will to stop the corporation's twisted vision for the future.

"We'll get the people we need," Lex said, his voice filled with determination. "We'll take them down, no matter the cost."

As the room fell silent, Lex knew one thing for certain: the battle had just begun. But this time, they had the upper hand.

And Omnitek wouldn't see them coming.

The safehouse was dark, save for the glow of computer

screens and the quiet hum of old servers still churning in the corner. Vex sat cross-legged on the floor, surrounded by maps and datapads, her focus entirely on planning their next move. Lex paced the room, his mind racing as he tried to process what Kane had told them.

Omnitek's plan to merge Eden with reality was more terrifying than anything they'd imagined. It wasn't just about controlling people's lives inside a virtual world; it was about erasing the line between the two, creating a hybrid existence where Omnitek held all the power.

"We're going to need more people," Lex said quietly, breaking the tense silence. "We can't do this with just a handful of hackers. Kane's right—we need an army."

Vex looked up from her work, her eyes shadowed with exhaustion. "I've been thinking about that. We have contacts, but it's not enough. Even if we rally every hacker and dissident we know, we'd still be outnumbered and outgunned."

Lex nodded, leaning against the wall. "Then we need to expand. We need to reach out to people who have influence, people who can help us turn this into something bigger."

Vex's brow furrowed. "You mean public figures? Politicians? We'd be risking everything if we went that route. Omnitek has eyes everywhere. They'll know what we're planning the moment we go public."

"Not if we do it right," Lex said, pushing away from the wall and pacing again. "There are people out there who want to bring Omnitek down, people who know what they're doing to the world but haven't had the chance to act. We give them that chance."

Kane, who had been quietly observing the conversation from the corner, spoke up. "You're talking about creating a movement. One that goes beyond hacking and digital resistance. You're talking about taking the fight to Omnitek on all fronts."

Lex nodded. "Exactly. We've been fighting from the shadows for too long. If we want to stop them, we have to expose them to the world. We need to show people what they're really doing with Eden."

Kane considered this for a moment, then stood. "I can get you names. People in the media, former executives, whistleblowers. But they're going to need proof. Something that will force them to act, something they can't ignore."

Vex looked over at Kane, her eyes narrowing slightly. "What do you suggest?"

Kane walked over to one of the old computer terminals and began typing, pulling up files from deep within Omnitek's archives. "I still have access to some of their internal data—sensitive information that could bring them down if it gets out. It's encrypted, but if you can crack it, you'll have what you need."

Lex stepped forward, glancing at the screen. The files Kane was pulling up were buried deep, hidden behind layers of security. If they could unlock them, it could be the smoking gun they needed to rally their allies.

"We'll get it," Lex said firmly. "Vex, can you work on decrypting this?"

Vex nodded, already moving toward the terminal. "I'll start now. But it's going to take time. This encryption is some of the strongest I've seen."

"Do whatever it takes," Lex said, turning back to Kane. "Once we have the data, we start reaching out. We need to get as many people on our side as possible before we make our move."

Kane crossed his arms, his expression serious. "And what about the facility? We can't afford to wait too long. Omnitek's not going to stop their work just because we're building an army."

Lex nodded. "We'll go after the facility as soon as we're ready. But we need to hit them where it hurts. If we can expose them publicly at the same time, we'll have the leverage we need to make sure they can't recover."

Vex glanced up from the terminal, her fingers flying over the keyboard. "I can reach out to some people in the media. Investigative reporters who aren't afraid to dig into corporate corruption. They've been looking for something like this—a story big enough to take down a giant like Omnitek."

"Good," Lex said, feeling the pieces start to fall into place. "Once we have the proof, we release it to the media and the public. We need to create enough pressure that Omnitek can't just sweep this under the rug."

"But we need to be careful," Kane warned. "Omnitek has resources we can't even imagine. If they find out what we're doing, they'll come after us with everything they have."

"We've been in hiding long enough," Lex replied. "It's time to stop running."

For the next several hours, they worked in silence, each of them focused on their task. Vex worked on decrypting the files, her brow furrowed in concentration, while Kane sorted through the data he still had access to, flagging anything that could be useful. Lex made lists of potential allies—people in the media, former Omnitek employees, politicians who had spoken out against corporate overreach. He knew it would take time to get them all on board, but he was prepared for the long fight.

As the night wore on, Vex suddenly let out a quiet exhale, her fingers pausing over the keyboard. "I'm in."

Lex moved quickly to her side, peering at the screen as the encrypted files began to unlock. The data within was staggering—documents detailing Omnitek's plans for Eden, their experiments on users, and their research into merging the virtual world with reality. It was everything they needed to expose the corporation's true intentions.

"This is it," Vex said, her voice filled with both awe and dread. "This is the proof."

Kane stepped forward, studying the files with a grim expression. "Release this, and Omnitek will be finished. But they'll fight back hard. You need to be prepared for that."

Lex nodded, feeling the weight of the moment. "We'll be ready. This is what we've been waiting for."

With the encrypted files unlocked, Lex and Vex began the process of reaching out to their contacts. It was a slow and cautious effort—they couldn't afford to make any mistakes. Every conversation was conducted in secret, every message encrypted to avoid detection. But little by little, their network began to grow. Journalists, whistleblowers, and even a few high-profile politicians started to rally behind the cause, their eyes opened to the true nature of Omnitek's plans.

Weeks passed, and the resistance swelled in size. What had once been a small group of hackers and rebels had grown into something far more powerful—a movement, ready to strike.

Lex stood in the center of the warehouse, watching as people moved in and out, preparing for the battle ahead. The data they had unlocked was being distributed to trusted media outlets, and soon the public would know the truth about Omnitek. The world was about to change, and Lex could feel the shift in the air.

"They're ready," Vex said, walking up beside him, her face set with determination. "Everyone's in place. The media's waiting for the signal, and the teams are prepped to move on the facility. All we need is your go-ahead."

Lex took a deep breath, his heart pounding. This was it. The moment they had been fighting for. The final step in their plan to take down Omnitek and stop their twisted vision for the future.

"Do it," Lex said, his voice steady. "Send the signal."

Vex nodded and stepped away to give the order. As she did, Lex felt a wave of resolve wash over him. This was what Jax and Maya had sacrificed their lives for. This was the moment they had all been fighting for.

As the message went out, Lex knew there was no turning back. The resistance was ready, their army assembled. Omnitek wouldn't know what hit them.

The fight for Eden—and for the future of reality itself—was about to begin.

The warehouse was humming with nervous energy. Every corner buzzed with quiet conversations, the sound of clicking keyboards, and the low hum of servers working overtime to ensure their communication lines were secure. Lex stood by the large digital map projected on the wall, his eyes scanning the various markers representing their teams spread across the city. This was it—the signal had been sent, and the final phase of their plan had begun.

Across from him, Vex monitored the transmissions coming in from their contacts, her fingers flying over the keys. Journalists were already mobilizing, prepping their stories and preparing to drop the bombshell on Omnitek's operations. The media had been given the proof, and now it was only a matter of hours before the world would know what Omnitek had been doing behind closed doors.

"Any word from our teams?" Lex asked, his voice steady but tense.

Vex glanced up at him. "So far, so good. They're in position around the facility, waiting for your order. Security is tighter than we expected, but they're ready."

Lex nodded, his mind racing through the final steps of the plan. They were on the verge of exposing Omnitek, but this was where it could all go wrong. The facility they were targeting—Omnitek's hidden lab—was the key to everything. If they could take it down, they could stop Omnitek's plan to merge Eden with reality once and for all. But the security around it was no joke, and they had no room for error.

Kane stood nearby, his arms crossed as he watched the map. "Omnitek knows something is happening. They'll be scrambling to contain this. We need to move before they can lock down the facility."

"Agreed," Lex said, his voice low. "Once we start, we hit fast and hard. We can't give them time to regroup."

The room fell silent for a moment as the weight of the impending operation settled over them. Lex could feel the tension in the air, the nerves of every person in the room starting to fray. They had come so far, sacrificed so much, and now they stood on the edge of a battle that could change everything. Lex thought of Jax, of Maya, of all the people who had fought and died for this moment. They couldn't afford to fail now.

Vex's voice cut through the silence. "We're getting reports from the media. The first stories are live. They're going public with the files now."

Lex felt a jolt of adrenaline. "What's the reaction?"

"It's spreading fast," Vex replied, scrolling through the reports. "Social media is already exploding with the news. People are in shock. Omnitek's stock is tanking, and we're seeing politicians and public figures starting to call for investigations. But Omnitek's not going to go down without a fight."

Lex knew she was right. The initial blow might have been dealt, but Omnitek wasn't just going to roll over. They still had their grip on Eden, and they still had the resources to retaliate. That's why the facility had to be taken down. If Omnitek managed to keep their lab operational, they could still proceed with their plans to merge Eden and reality, even in the face of public outrage.

"Is everyone in place?" Lex asked, his voice firm, trying to push back the nerves clawing at him.

"Yes," Vex confirmed, looking up from her screen. "Our teams are ready to breach. We're just waiting on your go."

Lex took a deep breath, feeling the weight of the moment. This was it—the moment where all their planning, all their sacrifices, would either pay off or fall apart. He thought of Maya's last words, her request that he finish what they'd started. He couldn't let her down. He couldn't let any of them down.

"Tell them to move in," Lex said, his voice steady. "Hit the facility and take down their systems. We end this today."

Vex nodded and sent out the final command. The room buzzed with activity as their teams received the order. Lex watched the map as the markers representing his people began to converge on the facility. His heart pounded in his chest, but his mind was clear. This was the only way to stop Omnitek. This was their last chance.

Minutes passed, feeling like hours, and the tension in the room continued to mount. Then, the first reports started coming in.

"Team Alpha is in," Vex said, her eyes scanning the feed. "No resistance so far. They're moving toward the main server room."

"Team Bravo is breaching the west entrance," another voice chimed in from across the room. "Encountering light security, but they're pushing through."

Lex exhaled slowly. So far, so good.

But then, just as the reports were coming in, an alarm sounded across the map. The facility was lighting up with activity—Omnitek's security forces were mobilizing, and the fight was about to get real.

"We've got incoming," Vex said, her voice tense. "Omnitek's private security is on the move. They're not going to let us take this place without a fight."

Lex stepped forward, his eyes locked on the map. "Tell our teams to hold the line. We need to secure the servers and destroy the core before Omnitek can reinforce. If they take control of the servers, we lose everything."

The room erupted into action as Lex's orders were relayed to the teams. On the screens, the fight began in earnest. His people were breaching the facility, taking down Omnitek's defenses, but the corporation was fighting back hard. Gunfire echoed through the comms, the sounds of chaos and battle filling the air as both sides clashed.

"Alpha is inside the server room!" one of the operators called out. "They're planting the charges now!"

Lex felt a flicker of hope. If they could destroy the core, Omnitek's plans would be shattered. But just as quickly as that hope appeared, it was crushed.

"Bravo team is pinned down!" Vex shouted, her eyes wide with alarm. "Omnitek's security reinforcements just arrived—they're overwhelming our people at the west entrance."

Lex's stomach twisted. They couldn't afford to lose Bravo team. If they were pinned down, Omnitek could lock down the facility and prevent them from reaching the core.

"I'm going in," Lex said suddenly, grabbing his gear and heading for the exit.

Vex looked up, alarmed. "Lex, no! You can't—"

"I have to," Lex cut her off. "If Bravo falls, the whole mission fails. I'm not letting that happen."

Vex hesitated, then nodded, knowing there was no stopping him. "Be careful," she said quietly.

Lex gave her a tight nod and ran out of the warehouse, his heart pounding in his chest. The streets were chaos as Omnitek's security forces swarmed the city, but Lex moved quickly, sticking to the shadows and avoiding detection. He reached the facility in minutes, the sounds of battle growing louder as he approached.

Inside, the scene was worse than he had imagined. Bravo team was pinned down behind cover, their weapons firing desperately as Omnitek's heavily armed security forces closed in. They were outgunned, and it was only a matter of time before they were overwhelmed.

Lex didn't hesitate. He rushed forward, joining the fight, taking out two of the security guards with quick, precise shots. Bravo team spotted him and rallied, fighting harder with renewed energy.

"Lex!" their team leader shouted over the gunfire. "We're holding, but we're not going to last much longer!"

"Get to the core!" Lex shouted back, moving toward cover. "I'll cover you!"

Bravo team didn't hesitate. They made a break for the server room, with Lex providing cover fire. The security forces pressed harder, but Lex held them off, his movements fast and calculated. He had been through too much to fail now.

Then, a massive explosion rocked the facility. The charges had gone off. The server room was destroyed.

Lex felt a wave of relief wash over him. They had done it. Omnitek's core was gone, their plans for Eden shattered.

The security forces began to retreat, their objective lost. Lex lowered his weapon, watching as his people regrouped.

"It's over," Lex said quietly, feeling the weight of it all settle over him.

Bravo's team leader walked up to him, breathless but smiling. "We did it."

Lex nodded, but his thoughts were already elsewhere. They had won the battle, but the war against Omnitek wasn't over. There would be more fights to come, more battles to be fought.

But for now, they had won. And it was enough.

The Fallout

The city was quieter than it had been in days. The constant hum of tension, the lingering anxiety that had gripped the streets, was finally beginning to subside. Lex stood on the roof of a building, overlooking the skyline as the first rays of morning sunlight cut through the fading darkness. For the first time in what felt like years, the air was still. The battle was over, the facility destroyed, and Omnitek's plans for Eden were shattered.

But Lex couldn't bring himself to feel the triumph that should have come with their victory. Yes, they had stopped Omnitek's immediate threat. The facility was gone, and the media storm had exposed the corporation's darkest secrets to the world. Public outrage had been swift and brutal—Omnitek's stock had plummeted, their executives were scrambling to control the damage, and government agencies had opened investigations into their practices. For now, the corporation was on the defensive, and that alone was a win.

Yet as Lex stared out at the city, a sense of unease gnawed at him. They had struck a heavy blow, but Omnitek wasn't finished. It was a massive entity, with roots that ran deeper than most could fathom. Taking down one facility, even one as critical as the lab they had destroyed, was just a step in a much larger war.

Behind him, Vex climbed up the stairs to the roof, stepping into the soft light of dawn. She looked exhausted, dark circles under her eyes from days without sleep, but there was a quiet strength in her that Lex had come to rely on.

"How's the team?" Lex asked, not taking his eyes off the horizon.

"They're recovering," Vex replied, coming to stand beside him. "We lost a few people, but most of us made it out. It could've been worse."

Lex nodded but didn't speak. The weight of those they had lost pressed down on him. Every life lost felt like a personal failure, even though he knew the risks had been high from the start. Still, the thought of Jax, of Maya, and now the others they had lost—it was almost too much to bear.

"We did it, you know," Vex said softly, glancing over at him. "We stopped them. The media's still going crazy with the story. Omnitek's getting hammered from all sides. They won't recover from this, not for a long time."

Lex finally turned to her, his expression serious. "Maybe. But they're not done, Vex. We hit them hard, but Omnitek is still out there. They're going to regroup, and they're going to come back stronger."

Vex sighed, leaning on the railing as she looked out over the city. "You're right. But we've shown them that we can fight back. We're not powerless. And now, we've got people on our side. The public knows what Omnitek's been doing. They won't be able to hide in the shadows anymore."

Lex couldn't argue with that. The public outrage had been overwhelming. People who had once trusted Omnitek implicitly were now questioning everything the corporation stood for. Lawsuits were piling up, and politicians who had once been in the company's pocket were now distancing themselves, trying to save face.

"They'll try to spin it," Lex said after a moment. "They'll claim they were rogue elements, that the executives didn't know what was really happening. They'll sacrifice a few people, throw them under the bus, and then they'll keep pushing forward, just with a new face."

Vex didn't disagree. "Maybe. But they're going to have to rebuild from the ground up. That's going to take time. We've given ourselves breathing room."

Lex exhaled, running a hand through his hair. He knew she was right, but it didn't feel like enough. After everything they'd been through, after everything they'd lost, the idea of Omnitek regrouping and coming back felt like a nightmare he couldn't escape.

"What now?" Vex asked quietly. "We've been fighting for so long. I'm not sure what comes next."

Lex looked down at his hands, flexing his fingers, still sore from the battle. What *did* come next? For years, all he had known was the fight against Omnitek, the constant struggle to expose the truth and take the corporation down. But now that they had dealt a serious blow, he felt... adrift.

"We keep fighting," Lex said finally. "But smarter this time. We've weakened them, but we need to stay vigilant. Omnitek's not going to disappear, and neither can we."

Vex nodded, though her expression was weary. "I know. But you need to take a break, Lex. We all do. You've been carrying this weight for too long."

Lex didn't respond right away, though he knew she was right. The fight had consumed him. It had taken everything—his friends, his sense of peace, and most days, his sense of self. He wasn't sure who he was without it.

"I don't know how to stop," Lex admitted quietly, his voice almost lost to the wind.

Vex looked at him, sympathy in her eyes. "You don't have to stop. But you need to rest. Just for a little while."

Lex met her gaze, and for the first time in what felt like years, he allowed himself to consider the idea of stepping back, even if only for a moment. The thought of rest felt foreign, almost impossible, but maybe it was what he needed.

"We'll figure out what comes next," Vex said gently. "Together."

Lex nodded, feeling a flicker of hope. The war wasn't over, but they had won a battle that mattered. For now, that had to be enough.

They stood there in silence for a while longer, watching the sun rise over the city. The light bathed the buildings in a soft, golden glow, and for the first time in a long while, Lex felt a sense of calm wash over him. The world was still broken, still teetering on the edge of chaos, but they had made a difference. They had fought back against the machine, and they had won.

For the moment, that was enough.

Finally, Vex spoke, breaking the silence. "When you're ready, there's something I want to show you."

Lex glanced at her, curious. "What is it?"

Vex smiled, a small but genuine expression. "It's a surprise. But it's important. Just... trust me."

Lex raised an eyebrow but nodded. "Alright. Lead the way."

As they descended the stairs from the roof, Lex felt a sense of cautious optimism. The fight wasn't over, but he wasn't alone in it. And for the first time in a long time, he felt like there might actually be a way forward.

As they walked through the quiet streets, Lex couldn't shake the feeling that the next chapter of their fight was about to begin.

And this time, they were ready.

Vex led Lex through the narrow streets, the early morning light casting long shadows on the ground. The tension from the battle had lifted slightly, but Lex could still feel the weight of everything they had been through. His mind buzzed with questions, but he trusted Vex enough to follow her in silence, wondering what she had to show him.

They weaved through alleyways and side streets until they reached an old, unmarked building. From the outside, it looked abandoned, like so many others in this part of the city. But Vex stopped in front of the door, pulling out a keycard from her jacket. She swiped it, and with a soft click, the door unlocked.

"After you," she said, giving Lex a small smile.

Lex hesitated for a moment, then stepped inside. The interior was a stark contrast to the worn-down exterior. Instead of dust and decay, the space was sleek, filled with advanced technology and equipment. Screens lined the walls, each one displaying data streams, maps, and surveillance footage. A handful of people were already inside, working quietly at terminals. It was clearly a command center, but for what?

"What is this?" Lex asked, turning to Vex.

She walked past him, moving deeper into the room. "This is our new headquarters. We've been building it for months, quietly, while we were planning the attack on Omnitek. It's off the grid, completely secure. No one knows about it except for a select few."

Lex raised an eyebrow. "And you didn't tell me?"

Vex chuckled softly. "We weren't sure how things would go with the facility. It wasn't the right time. But now... now it's time you see the bigger picture."

Lex followed her further into the room, past the rows of monitors and workstations, until they reached a large screen at the back of the room. Vex tapped a few keys, and the screen lit up, showing a detailed map of the entire city. Points of interest were marked in red, with lines connecting them like a web of digital threads.

"This is our new network," Vex explained. "We've been building it piece by piece, using the data we've collected over the past few years. We have eyes on Omnitek's remaining operations, as well as on other corporations trying to move into the same space. We're not just focusing on Eden anymore. We're looking at the bigger picture—at the systems and organizations that have been controlling everything from the shadows."

Lex studied the map, feeling the enormity of what they were undertaking. "This is a surveillance network?"

"Of sorts," Vex said. "But it's more than that. We've been reaching out to people—activists, dissidents, hackers, anyone who's been affected by these corporations. This isn't just about Omnitek anymore, Lex. We're building a movement, one that can challenge the entire system."

Lex's mind reeled. This wasn't what he had expected. They had always been focused on Omnitek, on Eden, on exposing the corporation's grip over the virtual and real worlds. But this—this was something else entirely. It was a plan to take down the very structures of power that had allowed Omnitek and others like it to thrive.

"You're serious about this," Lex said, half in awe.

Vex nodded, her expression solemn. "We have to be. Omnitek

was just the beginning. There are more like them—companies with too much power, governments turning a blind eye to corruption, systems built to control people rather than help them. We've been playing defense for too long. It's time to go on the offensive."

Lex stared at the map, his thoughts racing. He had always known their fight against Omnitek was part of something larger, but this... this was bigger than anything he had imagined. It wasn't just about one corporation or one system. It was about changing the way the world worked.

"This is... ambitious," Lex said finally, glancing over at Vex. "Do we even have the resources to pull something like this off?"

Vex smiled. "We have more than you think. Since the media exposé, people have been reaching out. Hackers, whistleblowers, even a few insiders from other corporations. The world is starting to wake up, Lex. They're starting to realize what's been happening behind the scenes. And they want to fight back."

Lex felt a flicker of hope. Maybe Vex was right. Maybe this wasn't just about surviving the next battle with Omnitek. Maybe this was about changing everything, about creating a future where people weren't at the mercy of faceless corporations and corrupt governments.

"So, what's the plan?" Lex asked, his voice steady.

Vex tapped the screen again, zooming in on several key points across the map. "First, we consolidate our network. We bring in as many people as we can—activists, journalists, anyone who can help spread the truth. We can't fight this battle alone, and we can't stay hidden forever. If we want to change things, we need to be seen. We need to make our presence felt."

Lex nodded, absorbing the enormity of the task ahead. It was risky, stepping into the light like this. They had always operated from the shadows, striking when Omnitek least expected it. But if they were going to truly challenge the system, they couldn't hide forever.

"And after that?" Lex asked.

Vex's eyes gleamed with determination. "After that, we start dismantling the power structures. One corporation at a time, one system at a time. We expose them, just like we did with Omnitek. We use the public outcry to force change, to bring down the people who've been pulling the strings."

Lex felt a strange sense of calm settle over him. For the first time in a long while, he could see the path ahead clearly. The battle with Omnitek had been brutal, and they had lost so much, but this—this was a chance to build something better.

"Alright," Lex said, turning to Vex. "Let's do it. Let's build the future we've been fighting for."

Vex grinned, her weariness momentarily forgotten. "I knew you'd come around."

As they stood together in the dimly lit command center, Lex felt the weight of the future pressing down on him. But for the first time, it didn't feel overwhelming. It felt possible.

They had fought against the machine, and they had won. Now, it was time to rebuild—not just for themselves, but for everyone who had been caught in the system's grip.

It wouldn't be easy. It wouldn't be quick. But Lex knew, deep down, that they could do it.

The future was theirs to shape, and they wouldn't stop until they had torn down the walls that had kept so many people trapped for so long.

For Jax. For Maya. For everyone.

In the days that followed, Lex felt a shift in the air. The quiet before the storm was over. The media exposé had unleashed a wave of public outrage, and the resistance was growing faster than anyone could have predicted. People from all corners of society—hackers, activists, former employees of Omnitek, and even ordinary citizens—were joining their ranks, eager to take a stand against the corporations that had controlled their lives for so long.

The warehouse, which had once been a quiet hub of resistance operations, was now buzzing with activity. New faces arrived every day, each one carrying stories of how they had been hurt or manipulated by Omnitek and other companies like it. They had all come for the same reason: to fight back.

Lex stood at the center of it all, watching as the movement took shape around him. Vex was at his side, coordinating the influx of new recruits and organizing the teams that would be crucial for the next phase of their mission. They had the people, they had the data, and now they had the momentum. But with that momentum came new challenges.

"The numbers are growing faster than we expected," Vex said, looking up from her terminal as she worked through another list of names. "We're going to need more resources—more secure locations, more equipment. If we don't manage this carefully, it could get out of control."

Lex nodded, his brow furrowed in thought. "I know. We need to make sure everyone coming in is vetted. Omnitek will try to infiltrate us, to send spies to undermine everything we've built."

"Already on it," Vex replied. "I've got a few trusted people working on background checks, running security sweeps on anyone who joins. But we're stretched thin, Lex. We've got people coming in from all over the country, even some from overseas. This is getting bigger than I think any of us anticipated."

Lex took a deep breath, letting the reality of their situation sink in. The movement was no longer just a small, underground resistance group. It was becoming something much larger—a full-blown revolution against corporate control. And with that growth came a level of responsibility Lex wasn't sure he was ready for.

But there was no turning back now. They had set things in motion, and the world was watching.

"We need to establish a clear leadership structure," Lex said, his voice firm. "This can't just be us calling the shots anymore. If this is going to work, we need people who can organize on a larger scale—people who can take charge of different regions, different parts of the network."

Vex glanced at him, raising an eyebrow. "You want to step back from leadership?"

Lex shook his head. "Not exactly. But this movement is too big for any one person to control. We need to decentralize, make sure that if Omnitek takes out one part of the network, the rest can still function. We can't afford to have a single point of failure."

Vex nodded slowly, her eyes thoughtful. "You're right. We'll start organizing the leadership cells—get people we trust in place to manage the different sectors. It'll give us more flexibility, but it also means we need to be careful about who we put in charge."

Lex leaned against the table, his gaze drifting over the room full of new recruits. "And we need to start training them. A lot of these people want to help, but they don't have the skills to fight a war like this. We need to make sure they're prepared."

"Already working on that too," Vex said with a small smile.

"We've got some of the best hackers and field operatives out there, and they're eager to teach. We'll start running training sessions—cybersecurity, tactical planning, everything they'll need to survive out there."

Lex felt a surge of gratitude for Vex. She was always one step ahead, always thinking through the details he might have missed. It was one of the reasons they had come this far.

"Good," Lex said. "Because we're going to need every advantage we can get."

As the hours passed, Lex moved through the warehouse, speaking with the new recruits, listening to their stories, and helping them find their place within the growing movement. Some were skilled hackers, eager to join the digital fight. Others had experience in organizing protests and rallies, and they were ready to take the fight to the streets. There were even a few former Omnitek employees, people who had seen the corporation's corruption firsthand and were now willing to risk everything to take them down.

One of the new recruits, a young woman named Kaida, caught Lex's attention. She was quiet, her eyes sharp and alert as she watched the activity around her. Lex had noticed her the moment she had walked in—there was something about the way she carried herself that set her apart from the others.

"You're Kaida, right?" Lex asked, approaching her.

She looked up, nodding. "That's right. I've heard a lot about you, Lex. You're the one who took down Omnitek's evolving code."

Lex gave a small, humble nod. "It wasn't just me. It was a team effort. We all played our part."

Kaida tilted her head slightly, studying him. "Still, it's impressive. I've been working against Omnitek for a while now, but nothing on the scale of what you pulled off. I'm here because I want to help. I have some skills you might find useful."

Lex raised an eyebrow. "What kind of skills?"

Kaida's eyes gleamed with quiet confidence. "Let's just say I know how to get into places I'm not supposed to be. Physical locations, secure buildings... I've been inside some of Omnitek's top facilities. And I've seen things—things that could help us take them down for good."

Lex's curiosity was piqued. "You're saying you've infiltrated Omnitek's secure sites?"

Kaida nodded. "I've spent the last few years moving from place to place, gathering intel. I didn't have the resources to do much with it before, but now that I'm here, I think I can be of real use to you."

Lex exchanged a glance with Vex, who had joined him. "If she's telling the truth, that kind of access could be invaluable," Vex said quietly.

Lex turned back to Kaida, nodding. "Alright. We'll give you a chance. We could use someone with your experience."

Kaida smiled faintly, her expression unreadable. "You won't regret it."

As Lex continued to speak with Kaida and the other recruits, he couldn't shake the feeling that this was the start of something far bigger than any of them had anticipated. The movement was growing faster than he had imagined, and with each new person who joined, they were one step closer to creating real, lasting change.

But with that growth came new risks. Omnitek wasn't going to sit back and let them build this resistance without fighting back. Lex knew they would retaliate, and when they did, it would be brutal.

"Keep an eye on her," Lex whispered to Vex as they walked away from Kaida. "She's valuable, but we need to be sure we can trust her."

Vex nodded. "I've already got her flagged for monitoring. If she's as good as she says, she'll be an asset. But if she's playing us, we'll know soon enough."

Lex felt a familiar tension in his chest. Trust was always in short supply, and the stakes were too high to take any chances.

As the day drew to a close, Lex returned to his place at the center of the room, watching as the movement continued to grow around him. He had never expected to be leading something this big, but now that they were here, he knew there was no going back.

This was the future they were fighting for—a future free from the control of corporations like Omnitek, where people had the power to shape their own lives. It wouldn't be easy, and the battles ahead would be harder than anything they had faced so far.

But for the first time, Lex truly believed they could win.

And that was enough to keep him moving forward.

It had been weeks since the resistance had truly begun to take shape. The steady hum of activity in the warehouse had transformed into an organized movement with dozens of cells working across the city and beyond. Every day, more people joined their cause, and Lex could feel the momentum growing. The movement was stronger than ever, and for the first time, they weren't just reacting to Omnitek—they were taking the fight to them.

But with every victory, Lex knew they were drawing closer to a tipping point. Omnitek had been quiet since the media exposé and the destruction of their hidden facility, too quiet. Lex had expected retaliation, a strike meant to cripple the movement before it grew too large. The silence had made him uneasy, and today, that silence would break.

Lex was at the main table, reviewing reports from the different cells, when Vex's voice cut through the air.

"Lex," she called, her tone sharp and urgent. "We've got a situation. You need to see this."

Lex moved quickly to where Vex stood, in front of a large screen displaying security footage from one of their safehouses. The feed was filled with chaos—figures in black combat gear storming the building, dragging people out, and tearing through their equipment. Omnitek's logo was stamped on the armor of the attackers.

"How did they find us?" Lex muttered, his heart sinking as he watched the scene unfold.

Vex's face was tight with frustration. "We don't know. This was one of our most secure locations, but they hit it hard, and they hit it fast. They knew exactly where to go."

Lex clenched his fists, anger boiling just beneath the surface. This wasn't just a raid—it was a message. Omnitek was done playing defense. They were coming for the resistance, and they weren't holding back.

"How many people were inside?" Lex asked, his voice low.

"Twenty," Vex replied, her tone grim. "We've lost contact with all of them. No one's answering their comms."

Lex's stomach twisted. Twenty people, gone in an instant, and they hadn't seen it coming. "We need to get those people back," he said, his voice hardening. "They're going to interrogate them, break them, and try to find out where the rest of us are."

"I know," Vex said, already pulling up more information on the screen. "We're working on a rescue plan, but Omnitek has tightened security. If we move too quickly, they'll ambush us."

Lex knew she was right. They couldn't afford to rush in without a plan, but the longer they waited, the more dangerous it became for their captured people.

"We'll get them out," Lex said, trying to steady himself. "But we need to figure out how they found the safehouse in the first place. Someone gave them that intel."

Vex frowned, her eyes narrowing. "You think we have a mole?"

"I don't know," Lex admitted. "But it's the only thing that makes sense. We've been careful. No one outside of a select few knew about that location."

Vex bit her lip, glancing around the room. "I'll start investigating. But if we have a mole, we need to move fast before they can feed Omnitek any more information."

Lex's mind raced. The possibility of a mole was terrifying. They had worked so hard to build trust within the movement, to create something that could stand against Omnitek, and now there was a chance that someone from the inside was betraying them.

"Focus on the rescue for now," Lex said, his voice firm. "I'll handle the mole situation. We can't let this tear us apart."

Vex nodded, her expression resolute. "I'll keep you updated. But Lex, be careful. If there's a traitor in our ranks, they'll be watching our every move."

Lex nodded, already feeling the weight of the situation pressing down on him. He turned and made his way toward the back of the warehouse, where Kaida was working quietly at one of the terminals. Her infiltration skills had been invaluable since she'd joined, and she had quickly proven herself to be one of the most capable members of the team.

"Kaida," Lex called, approaching her. "I need your help."

She looked up, her sharp eyes locking onto his. "What's going on?"

Lex quickly filled her in on the situation, watching her face for any sign of emotion. Kaida was always hard to read, but she listened intently, nodding as he spoke.

"You think someone's leaking information," Kaida said once he was finished.

"Yes," Lex replied. "We need to figure out who it is, and we need to do it quietly. If Omnitek has a mole, we can't let them know we're onto them."

Kaida leaned back in her chair, considering for a moment. "I can help with that. I've been monitoring communications between our cells, watching for anything unusual. I'll dig deeper, see if I can find any patterns that point to a leak."

Lex nodded, grateful for her quick thinking. "Good. But be careful. We don't know how deep this goes."

Kaida gave him a small smile, though her eyes remained serious. "I'm always careful, Lex."

As Kaida turned back to her work, Lex felt the tension in his chest tighten. They had come so far, but now the walls were closing in. Omnitek was making their move, and it felt like they were one step ahead.

Hours passed, and the warehouse was filled with the tense hum of activity. Vex worked on the rescue plan, coordinating with other cells to pull together the resources they needed to retrieve their captured people. Lex kept a close eye on the communication channels, looking for any sign of further attacks. His mind churned with questions—who was the mole? How long had they been feeding information to Omnitek? And how much damage had already been done?

Just as the sun began to set, Kaida approached him, her expression grim.

"I found something," she said quietly.

Lex's heart skipped a beat. "What is it?"

Kaida handed him a datapad, the screen displaying a series of encrypted messages. "I traced some unusual activity from one of our internal servers. Someone's been sending encrypted data outside our network. It's heavily disguised, but I managed to break through the encryption. The data was sent to an Omnitek-controlled node."

Lex's jaw tightened. "Who?"

Kaida hesitated, then pointed to a name on the screen. Lex's blood ran cold when he saw it.

It was someone he had trusted, someone who had been with the resistance since the beginning.

Lex felt the weight of betrayal settle over him, cold and sharp. "We need to bring them in. Now."

Kaida nodded, her expression unreadable. "I'll handle it."

As she turned to leave, Lex stared at the datapad, his mind swirling with a mixture of anger and disbelief. The enemy had struck back, but the real threat had been within all along.

Omnitek had played them perfectly.

And now, it was time to strike back.

The weight of the revelation pressed down on Lex like a crushing force. His mind swirled with disbelief, anger, and confusion as he stared at the name on the datapad. Someone he had trusted, someone who had fought beside them for months, had been feeding Omnitek information from the inside. The betrayal stung more than any of the battles they'd faced. This was personal.

Kaida had gone to intercept the traitor, and Lex found himself pacing back and forth, his mind racing with thoughts of what he would say—or do—once he confronted them. The warehouse buzzed with activity as the rest of the team prepared for the rescue mission, unaware of the dangerous undercurrent that was now threatening to tear the movement apart.

Minutes later, Kaida returned, leading the betrayer through the side entrance. Lex's heart pounded in his chest as he looked up and saw the familiar face of Ethan, one of the original members of the resistance. He had been there since the beginning, standing by Lex's side as they plotted to take down Omnitek. Now, that same person had been working to destroy everything they had built.

"Ethan," Lex said, his voice low but filled with barely contained fury. "Tell me it isn't true."

Ethan's eyes darted around the room, his expression a mix of fear and defiance. "Lex, listen to me, I—"

"No," Lex interrupted, stepping forward. "No excuses. No lies. I want the truth. You've been feeding information to Omnitek, haven't you?"

Ethan opened his mouth to respond but hesitated. His silence was all the confirmation Lex needed.

"I trusted you," Lex continued, his voice growing louder. "We all trusted you. And you've been selling us out to the very people we're fighting against."

Ethan's face contorted with guilt and desperation. "I didn't have a choice, Lex. They found me—they threatened my family. If I didn't give them what they wanted, they would've killed them. What was I supposed to do?"

Lex stopped in his tracks, his anger momentarily tempered by the weight of Ethan's words. He knew what Omnitek was capable of, the lengths they would go to in order to control people. But betrayal, even under duress, was still betrayal. The damage Ethan had caused was undeniable.

"You should have come to me," Lex said, his voice strained. "We could've protected you. We could've found another way."

Ethan shook his head, his eyes brimming with frustration. "You don't understand, Lex. It wasn't just about me. They have resources we can't even imagine. They knew everything about my life—my wife, my kids. I couldn't risk it. I didn't want to hurt anyone here, but I didn't see a way out."

Kaida stepped forward, her voice sharp. "And how long were you planning on letting them string you along, Ethan? How many more of us were you going to sacrifice to keep your secret?"

Ethan looked down, his shoulders slumping under the weight of his guilt. "I tried to give them as little as possible, just enough to keep them off my back. I never meant for it to go this far."

"Twenty people," Lex said coldly. "Twenty people are in Omnitek's hands right now because of you."

Ethan flinched at the number, his face pale. "I didn't know they were going to hit the safehouse. I swear, Lex, I didn't know."

Lex felt the anger rising again, a sharp, burning feeling in his chest. He wanted to lash out, to make Ethan understand the gravity of what he had done. But he knew that anger wouldn't solve anything. They needed to be smart. There was too much at stake.

"Right now, I don't care why you did it," Lex said, his voice cold but controlled. "What I care about is fixing this. You're going to tell us everything you've told Omnitek. Every detail. And then you're going to help us get our people back."

Ethan swallowed hard, nodding slowly. "I'll do whatever it

takes to make this right."

Lex turned to Kaida. "Get him in front of a terminal. I want every piece of information he's given them. We need to know exactly what we're up against."

Kaida gave a quick nod, grabbing Ethan by the arm and leading him toward one of the workstations. As they moved away, Lex took a deep breath, trying to steady himself. The betrayal cut deep, but there wasn't time to dwell on it. They had people to save, and every second they delayed brought their captured teammates closer to breaking.

Vex approached him, her expression grim. "I heard what happened. You think we can trust him to cooperate?"

Lex hesitated, glancing over at Ethan as Kaida began questioning him. "I don't know. But we don't have a choice. If we're going to pull this off, we need him."

Vex nodded, her face tightening with worry. "We're ready for the rescue mission. But if Omnitek knows we're coming, it's going to be a bloodbath."

"We'll have to move fast," Lex said, his voice hardening. "If Ethan's information checks out, we'll know where they're holding our people and how to get them out. But we can't trust that Omnitek hasn't set a trap."

Vex sighed, rubbing her forehead. "It's a risk we'll have to take."

Lex clenched his fists, feeling the weight of the decision pressing down on him. This wasn't how he had wanted things to go. They had been making progress, growing stronger, and now Omnitek had managed to strike them from the inside.

But Lex wasn't going to let this betrayal tear the resistance apart. Not now. Not when they had come so far.

"Get the teams ready," Lex said, turning to face Vex. "We

move as soon as we have the intel."

Vex nodded and hurried off to begin preparations. Lex watched her go, feeling the tension rise again. They were walking into a trap—he could feel it—but there was no other choice. They had to save their people. They had to stop Omnitek from tearing them apart.

As Lex stood alone in the center of the warehouse, watching the activity unfold around him, he felt the familiar weight of leadership pressing down on him. Every decision he made carried the lives of his people with it. One wrong move, and more of them would die.

But this wasn't about second-guessing himself anymore. This was about survival.

Lex had trusted Ethan, and that trust had been broken. Now, all he could do was pick up the pieces and keep moving forward.

And when the time came, Lex would make sure Omnitek paid for every life they had taken.

Milton Keynes UK
Ingram Content Group UK Ltd.
UKHW020001231024
449917UK00010B/459